W9-BNU-697

Till
Morning
Is NIGH

A WORTHAM FAMILY CHRISTMAS NOVELLA

Till Morning *Is* NIGH

Leisha Kelly

Revell
Grand Rapids, Michigan

© 2007 by Leisha Kelly

Published by Fleming H. Revell
a division of Baker Publishing Group
P.O. Box 6287, Grand Rapids, MI 49516-6287

Printed in the United States of America

ISBN 978-0-8007-1887-9

To my parents,
who made Christmases merry
with far more love than money.

In loving memory of my father,
and with continuing thanks to you, Mom,
for your undying support and, for this book, your recipe
help above and beyond the call to duty.

And also to Justice and Hosanna,
the originators of the "traveling" nativity set. You are a
blessing and a joy. I love you always.

Away in a Manger

Away in a manger, no crib for a bed,

The little Lord Jesus laid down his sweet head;

The stars in the sky looked down where he lay,

The little Lord Jesus, asleep on the hay.

The cattle are lowing, the baby awakes,

But little Lord Jesus, no crying he makes;

I love thee, Lord Jesus! Look down from the sky,

And stay by my cradle till morning is nigh.

Be near me, Lord Jesus, I ask thee to stay

Close by me forever, and love me, I pray;

Bless all the dear children in thy tender care,

And take us to heaven, to live with thee there.

Away in a Manger

December 1932

I heard the sounds of tramping feet and youthful voices floating across our winter-barren farmyard before they even got close to the porch. Hammond children were up and out and practically on our doorstep early, the way they were on so many school day mornings. As they neared, I could distinguish only two of the voices easily: baby Emmie fussing in distress and four-year-old Berty belting out a woefully off-key Christmas carol. I told Sarah and Katie to finish their breakfast and then glanced out the window at the children outside. Nine of the ten neighboring Hammond youngsters. Only the oldest boy, Sam, who had gone off to Farmington for a couple of months to work for an uncle, wasn't with them. Seeing them in their ragged coats and worn old shoes made me sigh. Sixteen-year-old Lizbeth carried the baby. Next to her, fourteen-year-old Joe held Berty's hand, and the rest all clustered around them except Franky, with his frightful limp, who struggled along several paces behind. Of course it was normal for boys and girls to walk a mile or more to school, and even to stop along the way at the houses of friends. But it pained me for them to have to bring the little ones out, now that the weather had gotten cold, and for Franky to have to walk so far when he struggled so much with his leg.

"Jus' keep Franky an' the little ones with you over-nights," their father had told me. "You could keep all of 'em through the week if you want. You's a mite closer to the schoolhouse anyway."

But maybe precisely because he was so anxious for that, Lizbeth was dead set against it. "We oughta stay with Pa 'cause we're family," she'd insisted several times. "We gotta stay together. It ain't so bad to walk."

And Franky, bravely agreeing with her, was home over-night most of the time now too, though he'd stayed with us much of the summer and fall at his father's request after suffering a badly broken leg.

So many concerns jumbled around in my head this sea-son, about Christmas coming on and how the Hammond children would bear the first anniversary of their mother's passing. About the baby having to venture out with them into the cold this winter. And about nine-year-old Franky, who sometimes seemed weaker now than the rest. My ag-gravation mounted at George Hammond for not keeping any of his children with him now that he wasn't harvest-ing. But on days when any of the younger ones stayed at home, Lizbeth had to miss school to be with them. George simply would not watch his little ones by himself.

I turned from the window and saw Katie staring morosely down at her breakfast bowl. She'd been so quiet lately. I wondered for her sake too. If we didn't hear anything from her mother, it would be their first Christmas apart. And though Katie hadn't said a word about it, I feared it was troubling her much more than she let on.

Robert jumped up and threw a chunk of wood into the stove for me just as the Hammonds' footsteps sounded on the porch outside. They didn't bother knocking. They never did anymore. I cleared a few dishes from the table as they burst into our kitchen, bringing chilly puffs of December air along with them.

"Mrs. Wortham." Lizbeth called my attention immediately, shifting her baby sister in her arms. "I'm awful sorry to bring Emmie Grace over fussy. I think she might be feverin', an' I didn't wanna take her out, but Pa said you'd know better'n us what to do."

He could have just sent for me! I thought immediately. *I would have met them at their house, saving Lizbeth, Franky, and the baby a mile walk through the timber!*

But I didn't speak my thoughts aloud. They were here now, and needed my calm assurance. I moved quickly and took the baby into my arms.

Little Berty tapped his feet on the kitchen floor and lifted his voice again. "Lidda Lor' Jesus lay down his sweet head!"

His older brother Willy nudged him, but Berty kept right on singing until six-year-old Harry gave him a shove and started chasing him around the table.

"I'm awful sorry," Lizbeth repeated. "I offered to stay home from school with Emmie today, but Pa says he's sore from a slip on our back steps, an' he'd get along better without us over there right now. I can stay here an' help you with her if you want me to." Harry and Bert whizzed past her, and she made a grab for Harry's coat collar, missing by inches. "Boys! Quit yer ruckus!"

She looked so tired. I didn't relish the idea of tending to a sick toddler today, but Lizbeth was only sixteen and shouldn't have to carry as much as she did for her younger brothers and sisters. "No," I told her quickly. "Your father's right that you should go on to school. Franky will help me, won't you, Franky?"

He looked up as though my words had jarred him out of some faraway thought. "Yes, ma'am?" he asked, and I knew he hadn't really heard anything but his name.

Before I could reply, Bert bumped against my leg trying to get away from Harry, and fourteen-year-old Joe grabbed both little boys and plopped them into the nearest chairs. Sarah and Katie picked up their dishes and moved away from them.

"You gotta help Mrs. Wortham with Emmie today," Lizbeth admonished Franky. He was still leaning against the wall near the door, where he'd stopped to catch his breath when they first came in, and he nodded without a single question or complaint.

"Lidda Lor' Jesus!" Berty piped up again. "As'eep on da hay!"

"Shut up," Willy grouched at him.

"Willy, mind your manners," I said. "Have you all eaten?" Several heads nodded assent, but I knew the big boys would gladly eat more. Lizbeth was the cook at their house now, and she had a terrible time fixing enough for all of her brothers. My eleven-year-old, Robert, could eat like a horse sometimes, but nothing to rival these Hammond boys. "We've had cornmeal mush," I told them. "There's more in the pot if anyone's hungry."

Thirteen-year-old Kirk moved immediately to help himself, followed by eleven-year-old Willy. Joe glanced over at the cuckoo clock. "We got time?"

"Plenty," I told him. "You're early again."

I knew the Hammonds came early on purpose. As often as possible. Whether it was because the children were always anxious to be on their way or their father was anxious to have them gone, I wasn't sure. But they were early far more often than not, and spent a lot of other time with us besides.

I'd been keeping three of the Hammond children on a regular basis while the rest were in school, mostly so Lizbeth could continue to attend. Bert and Emmie, of course, because they were too young to go. But also Franky, because the teacher at our one-room schoolhouse had requested that he not attend this year. She said she was exhausted after three years of trying to get him through the first primer, and working with a child so slow was a hindrance and a distraction to all the learning she was trying to promote in her other students. I worked with Franky here, though his father thought I was wasting my time. But I knew Franky was bright, despite what anyone said, so I'd borrowed books to do what I could for him.

Joe joined Kirk and Willy in claiming some of the leftover mush, and I thanked the good Lord for our generous sack of cornmeal. My husband didn't like mush very well, but it was an inexpensive way to fill the pot for so many. That was important right now. It had been months since Samuel had had work outside of our farm, and we had no money left for anything. We were far from alone in that. There seemed to be no jobs at all in our area. Everybody we knew was struggling, including the Hammonds, even though the oldest boy sent money when he could.

Harry and Bert weren't interested in eating, and as soon as they saw that Joe's attention was elsewhere, Bert dove under the table with Harry hot on his heels. Poor little Emmie Grace let out another miserable wail. I gently unwrapped the blanket Lizbeth had tucked around her and took off her little knitted cap and coat.

"She does seem warm," I said, wondering if she was hurting anywhere. But Emmie was nineteen months old and not talking well enough yet to tell us very much.

"I kinda hate to leave her when she ain't feelin' well," Lizbeth said, and I tried to assure her it would be all right to go on to school. Emmie would be fine here with me. Reluctantly, Lizbeth agreed to go, but only because she didn't want to miss the important tests today.

I wished their father took as much care with the children as Lizbeth did. In the back of my mind, I wondered what my Samuel would think when he got home. We'd talked about this, about George Hammond being so quick to shove his children in our direction and whether it was really right to let him do it. But we'd learned from experience how miserable it was for these kids at home when he didn't want them there. It was enough to make me want to keep them whenever I could. Especially the little ones and Franky, who seemed to need so much that George couldn't, or wouldn't, give.

I wondered if George had really fallen on the steps and gotten hurt like he'd told Lizbeth, or if there was something else to his wanting to be alone today. I prayed he was all right, but with the anniversary of his wife's death coming so soon upon us, I worried. Surely he realized how hard this must be for the children too.

Bert started singing his carol all over again, failing to notice that nobody else displayed any enthusiasm for it. "Away in a manger . . ."

I'd sung it with the children in Sunday school last week, but I'd had no idea it would stick in Berty's mind so.

"Stop it!" Willy growled at him again. "I tol' you an' tol' you, I don't wanna hear no more Christmas songs!"

Those words, spit out in barely contained fury, worked painfully at my insides. It was easy to see the anger churning so prominently in Willy's eyes. But it seemed to be melancholy working in Joe, who answered quickly with his voice low and somber. "*You* stop it, Will. He's jus' a little kid. He don't know no better."

Lizbeth didn't speak to either of them. She seemed to be doing her best to ignore Bert's boisterous carol as well as the reaction it had gotten. "I tried to get some breakfast down her," she said, talking about Emmie again, "but she didn't want nothin'. Didn't drink much neither."

"I'll try again," I assured her. "Maybe just some water for now."

The big boys polished off most of the rest of the mush and set their bowls and spoons in the dishpan.

"Sarah, Katie, get your books," I called, cradling Emmie

13

in one arm and reaching for lunch pails with the other. Robert was pulling on his coat and hat, and Harry went searching under the table for a fallen mitten.

"It's gonna snow," Kirk announced gloomily.

Nobody acknowledged the words with anything more than a look. I didn't address them either. Snow was the last thing I wanted to think about right now.

I suddenly realized I hadn't heard a peep out of Rorey, the only other Hammond girl. She was just a little older than my seven-year-old, Sarah, and usually one of the loudest of the bunch. But today she'd stepped in quietly without a word. She was sitting sideways in one of the chairs, not looking quite herself.

"Rorey, are you feeling all right?"

She shook her head. I walked to her quickly to feel whether she was as warm as her little sister, but before I got there, she suddenly pitched forward and lost her unidentifiable breakfast all over the floor.

"Ewww!" Harry shouted.

I handed the baby to Joe and tried my best to clean Rorey up a little. Sure enough, she was feverish too.

"Are any of the rest of you feeling poorly?" I asked with a sinking feeling. Oh, what terrible timing!

"I wish," Willy answered me glumly. "I don't want no tests today."

"Can I lie down?" Rorey asked me miserably.

"I'll wash the floor," Lizbeth offered, so I went with both of the little girls into our bedroom. Rorey climbed up on the bed, and I tried to lay Emmie down too, but she didn't want to let go of me.

"I don't wanna be sick," Rorey told me.

14

"I don't blame you, honey. And I'm so sorry."

"I wish I didn't get out of bed today."

"You can stay right in this bed for awhile. It's all right. Were you feeling poorly when you first got up?"

She nodded, sinking into the pillows and looking miserable.

Maybe Lizbeth had been too busy with Emmie to realize that Rorey was sick too. Maybe Rorey hadn't even tried to tell anyone. I didn't know. But she shouldn't have been sent out in the cold, that was for sure.

Rorey sniffed, tears filling her eyes. "I hate winter! It's always full of bad stuff."

"Oh, honey. There's a lot of good too."

Emmie fussed so much I really couldn't console Rorey. Emmie wouldn't lie down. She only wanted to be held, but even though I obliged her, she continued to fuss. And the rest of the kids needed to scurry on to school now. Rorey shut her eyes, and I knew she was ready to rest. I took Emmie with me to get Rorey a glass of water, and then I turned my attention to getting the other little girls and everybody else on their way.

I made Katie and Sarah pull on double stockings and bundle up against the chill. Neither of them had boots that fit, but we could be thankful that their sturdy shoes would last them through the winter.

"It just figures that somebody'd get sick in December," Willy said. "Just like Mama and Emma Graham last year."

Such a thought left everybody quiet. Both women had died just days before Christmas.

It was a sullen group of children that left my house for

school that morning. Even Katie, who hadn't been with us a year ago to understand the losses that had hit us so hard, seemed sullen and preoccupied. *Lord, be with us. We can't help but think about it! How are we ever going to get through Christmas?*

I watched at the window for a moment as four Hammond boys, along with Lizbeth, Robert, Sarah, and little Katie trudged across the farmyard with their lunch pails and books in hand. Lizbeth wouldn't have left at all, except for my promise that I'd be fine tending to Rorey and Emmie without her. But it was more than the little girls' sickness on my mind. Only ten days until the holiday was upon us. What on earth was the matter with me that I hadn't been doing more to prepare these children, to start sharing holiday blessings with them? No wonder they seemed so down in the mouth, even my own children. They must all be wondering what Christmas would hold for them this year, when we were still so aware of the empty places inside us. Wilametta Hammond, mother of ten. And dear old Emma Graham, my precious friend. Both gone in one awful, frigid night.

But I could not stop to dwell on such things now. With a sigh, I turned from the window to face the four little Hammonds still here with me. I almost wished I could have kept all the children home longer, perhaps for a game or some holiday baking, anything to bring a smile to their faces before they had to head out in the cold. But there would be time for that, though I'd been putting it off too long. I needed to bring out the decorations, immerse the children in all the holiday cheer I could muster. Samuel had even told me the same thing. "As hard as it is for all of us," he'd said, "they're going to need all the Christmas we can give them this year."

Of course he was right, but we had precious little to give. All of the Hammonds would be at our house again. That was an agreement Samuel had already made with George, who insisted that he couldn't handle Christmas at all without our help. He'd promised to bring a ham. We were making presents. But those would not be the important things. We would need a touch from God this year to find healing, to find real peace.

"Lidda Lor' Jesus," Berty was singing under the table. "As'eep on da hay."

At least there was one of us in the Christmas spirit. Emmie tugged a strand of my hair loose as I put the teakettle on to heat. Maybe some mild chamomile tea sweetened with a touch of honey would be of benefit to both girls. Or willow bark, to cut the fever.

Franky must have been thinking along the same lines. "You got medicine?"

"I've got a few things. But rest is probably what they need most."

"Rorey's a'ready asleep. That's good, ain't it?"

I hadn't noticed him going to check on her. "Yes, that's good. Hopefully she can sleep several hours. It'd be the best thing for her."

"She bad sick?" Berty suddenly asked, the uncertainty plain in his eyes.

"I don't think it's bad, no."

"Like Mama sick?"

"No. Nothing like that. She'll be just fine. Don't worry." It was easy to assure him, and he quickly turned his

17

thoughts to our regular routine. "We do school today?" He ran for the drawer that held Crayolas. Berty had felt left out when Harry started school without him this year, so I always gave him something to do when I worked with Franky. That satisfied him that they both "did school" at our house.

"You can color me a picture to go along with that lovely song you were singing," I told him. "Then after I get Emmie to eat something, or at least drink aplenty, we can start something else."

"Okay," he answered me, reaching into the cupboard for paper.

"You usually wash the breakfast dishes first," Franky observed. "Do you want me to do that for you?"

I hesitated. But he was already started across the kitchen. He dipped warm water into the dishpan from the large pot I'd set at the back of the stove before breakfast.

"Where's the soap?" he asked me.

I reached for a cake of Alberta Mueller's homemade lavender lye hand soap from the cupboard. "This is the only kind I have left. I was going to grate just a bit. But the dishes can wait—"

"Oh, I'll grate it for you," he offered immediately. "I like to grate soap. Lizbeth lets me do that a lot."

I smiled. Franky always wanted to keep busy and stay helpful. He'd been that way even when his leg was bothering him the most and he couldn't do outside chores like the other boys. And Lizbeth had gotten very good at finding small tasks that gave him an opportunity to contribute. "Wonderful," I told him. "That will be a great help."

I tried to interest Emmie in the last dab of mush. Nothing

18

doing. I tried a little applesauce, and she wouldn't take more than three bites. She didn't want milk either, but she did drink water for me, a good half a cup, and that was a relief.

Rorey slept most of the morning, but I couldn't get Emmie to sleep at all, so she was cranky as a little bear by the time Samuel came home around lunchtime. Our neighbor, Barrett Post, had come early in the morning for Samuel's help with his furnace, and I'd prayed they could get it in good working order quickly. Louise Post had been down with the flu, and I knew she needed the heat.

Samuel gave me a kiss and told me they'd managed to get the furnace fixed all right. "Looks like you've had your hands full," he said and lifted Emmie from my arms.

"Constantly. She hasn't tolerated me putting her down for more than a minute all morning." Then I told him about Rorey in our bed with a fever and George over at their house resting alone after slipping on their back steps.

Samuel shook his head. "You'd think Lizbeth would have wanted to stay home with all three of them."

"She would have. But George wouldn't let her."

Samuel frowned. "I'll go talk to him after lunch. Maybe he just wanted your doctoring help with the girls, without troubling you to come out."

"Maybe." I certainly wasn't convinced, and Samuel knew my doubts. He had enough understanding of George to have plenty of doubts of his own. "I'll send some liniment with you when you go over there," I told him. "And a bite to eat too, in case he hasn't stirred around to get himself anything."

"Six, seben . . ." Berty's voice, quiet with concentration,

floated in from the sitting room. I'd given him and Franky each a bowl of dried beans to use for an arithmetic lesson. Berty was just to line his up and see how high he could count. But Franky had a much different assignment: find out how many beans in his bowl and divide the number by five, and then by twelve. I hoped it wasn't too difficult for him. Berty kept up his counting aloud, but Franky didn't make a sound.

I turned my attention to fixing lunch, and Samuel sat at the kitchen table with Emmie in his arms. "Barrett said he couldn't pay me for the help today," he said with a sigh. "Things are bad when even the Posts can't pay. He said he'd return the favor when he could."

I counted potatoes, trying to decide how many we'd use with Rorey and Emmie not likely to have very big appetites. "That's all right. That's what neighbors are for." But despite my words, I felt a familiar uneasiness stirring inside me. We were facing the holidays again absolutely penniless.

Even without looking his way, I knew Samuel was watching me. "I've been working on some ideas for a few of the boys," he told me, his voice barely above a whisper. "Have you been able to make much progress toward gifts?"

"Some. Not enough yet."

"There's time. We'll have something for everyone before the holiday."

I plopped potatoes in a pot, jackets and all. Something for everyone? Oh, there was so much more to Christmas than the gifts! But he was right. We had to make do. "I've been working on a blouse for Lizbeth. And a doll for Katie."

"Any ideas for the oldest boys?"

I wasn't sure what to tell him. But a shuffle of footsteps coming in from the sitting room interrupted our conversation anyway.

"There was a hun'erd an' eighty-nine beans in my bowl, Mrs. Wortham," Franky announced. "Dividin' out fives makes thirty-seven with four lef' over. An' dividin' out dozens gives fifteen, leavin' nine."

I stared at him for a moment. He'd gotten done far more quickly than I expected. It took me a while thinking that through before I could answer him with a nod. "You're right. That was very good."

"Excellent figuring, Franky," Samuel congratulated him. "You've made great progress with your arithmetic."

The boy acknowledged the compliment with barely a nod. "You don't hafta fix me up nothin' for Christmas," he told my husband immediately. "I got a pocketknife from your brother in July, and there weren't nobody else got a present back then."

Samuel shook his head. "He gave that to you because he felt terrible about hitting you with his car. That's something different."

"It was still a present. An' I sure have liked it too. So I'm satisfied with nothin' else this year if we're comin' up short. All I need's some wood to whittle on regular, an' that's easy to come by 'round here."

I didn't know what to say. I could almost picture us wrapping up a pile of sticks for his Christmas gift, which really would suit him. He took to working wood even better than he took to dividing beans.

"Now, Franky," Samuel said. "It's not your job to be

worrying over gifts. All right? The Lord will provide for our needs."

Franky nodded, suddenly seeming far more grown up than his years. "But he uses people often as not, and I a'ready heard 'bout people's hands bein' empty this year. Mr. Willis said he don't remember a time in his whole life when things was this bad. So I know his wife an' the other church folks can't send us stuff like they did last year to make us feel better 'bout things."

"Would you like to help me set the table?" I asked him, hoping to change the subject. His talk of gifts, and especially about last year, was making me uncomfortable. He pushed a chair toward the cupboard, but I really didn't want him climbing on it to reach the plates, so I passed them down to him.

"I know somethin' Pa needs," he said suddenly.

"What?" I asked him in spite of myself.

"Some new hankies. He ain't got hardly a one without holes in it no more."

I might have expected almost anything coming from Franky, who knew very well about his father's struggles. But this was a very practical suggestion. And workable. I thanked him.

Rorey got up for lunch, feeling some better. She even ate a tiny amount and seemed to have no trouble holding it down. And her fever was gone. Emmie, on the other hand, was just as restless, feverish, and fussy as she was when they'd first gotten here that morning.

"Do you need me to go and get the doctor?" Samuel asked.

It wasn't easy to answer. "I hate to call him out here. I

22

really do. But maybe we should, just to be safe." I could feel my eyes suddenly teary, and I got up to fetch Samuel a second cup of coffee, mostly so I could turn away from the children for a moment.

Bitter memories rushed over me like a flood. Of Wila and dear old Emma both sick. And me in my helplessness stranded with them at the Hammonds' in a snowstorm while the oldest Hammond boy, Sam, was missing for hours trying to get through to the doctor. Oh, how I hated the thought of someone sick in the winter again! I even hated winter now. I'd never, ever felt the barren coldness of it so much before.

"I'll check on George and borrow one of his horses," Samuel told me.

"Mr. Post's truck would be faster getting to town," I suggested, "if he'd let us borrow it again."

I turned back around with Samuel's coffee, and he was looking at me with a tender concern. "He probably would, under the circumstances. I hate to ask, but I believe he'd understand. I'll go there first and then get George on the way back from town. He ought to be here when the doctor comes."

I didn't like to see him leave again, and yet at the same time, I was relieved with the thought of having the doctor's opinion. Emmie being sick was scaring me, even though it didn't seem to be anything serious. Just the idea made me tense inside, and the longer it went on—even just part of this one day—the worse I felt. God help us. It's so foolish to overreact!

I knew it would be quite awhile before Samuel got back. We didn't have a vehicle, except the old tractor, or any horses of our own. Samuel would have to walk a mile and a half over to the Posts, then drive eight miles into town, and then stop and get George besides. Rorey and Franky helped me clear the table, but they were both very solemn. Maybe the doctor being called was enough to bother them too. Emmie wailed in my arms and refused my every attempt to get any medicine tea down her. I moved to the rocker in the sitting room, trying to console her. And Berty, who'd gotten quiet only toward the end of lunch, suddenly crowded onto my lap with her and lay his head against my shoulder.

"Hurts," he whispered.

"What hurts?"

"Dat ear I got," he proclaimed, without pointing to either one. "Hurts inside."

For a moment I thought this could be nothing more than a ploy for sympathy because Emmie'd had so much of my attention today. But then I noticed the tears in his big brown eyes, and I felt like crying too. Another child ill. And every single one of the others surely exposed! How many more would be sick before this was done?

Little Lord Jesus

I had to do something to get the children's minds off sickness. It was bad enough that they knew we were fetching the doctor. I didn't want them dwelling on it. I didn't want them scared. So even though Emmie and Berty were feeling far from perky, I tried my best to interest them all in singing a song with me. I thought Berty's Christmas carol would be a good choice, but Rorey was not in the mood to cooperate.

"Do we have to sing that?"

"I suppose we could sing a different song. How about 'Silent Night'?"

"I don't wanna sing," Rorey complained. "Pa says Christmas won't never be the same without Mama. So it won't be no good this year. He says people just gave us stuff last year because they felt sorry for us."

"Our church family brought food and gifts because they love all of you," I told her. "But if they aren't able to do that this year, it's because times are hard, not because they love you any less. And Christmas isn't about the presents anyway."

She crossed her arms and huffed at me a little. "Pa said you'd prob'ly try to act cheerful an' all—like ever'thin's dandy, but he'd ruther jus' skip holidays if he could."

"He spoke like that right in front of all of you?"

She shrugged. "Not all, I guess. I think Berty an' Emmie was sleepin' then."

I had to sigh. No wonder the Hammond kids had all seemed so glum. What they must be hearing all the time! I'd been far too reluctant to face the holidays myself. We couldn't go on like this. These children shouldn't go through any more days carrying around such gloomy thoughts instead of Christmas joy. "You know what?" I answered Rorey brightly. "It's high time we got into the Christmas spirit around here. We have decorating to do, and so much baking. We're going to have to get started this very day."

Berty looked at me with a tiny smile, but Rorey turned her head and stared out the window. "Kirk says not even you can make things right without Mama, Mrs. Wortham. Not at Christmas."

I sighed. "Probably not. But the Lord can still bless all of us, and we can do our best to honor him in this season. Besides," I tried to entice her, "we can have a little fun. You like cookies, don't you? We'll need to make a lot of cookies. Shaped like candy canes and trees and stars like last year."

"An' angels," Franky added.

"Yes. And I'll need lots of help."

Rorey didn't look convinced. She crossed her arms and stared at me. "Sarah can help when she gets home."

"What are you going to be doing?" I asked gently.

"I'll jus' watch. Maybe. Anyhow, I dunno if I can even eat no cookies nohow. Maybe my tummy'll get sick all over again."

"I think you're going to be fine. And you might decide to help. You might as well if you're going to be close enough to watch us. Which kind of cookie is your favorite?"

She frowned, but she didn't hesitate to give me an answer. "The candy canes, 'cause you gots to use red sugar. You still got any red sugar?"

"I have plenty of red coloring," I told her, though I knew very well that we'd be sorely in need of sugar before long. I had so hoped that Mr. Post would be able to pay Samuel even just a few cents today. But if there was no other way, perhaps we could take a few eggs into the grocer in trade. The Lord would provide. My grandma Pearl and dear old Emma Graham had told me that so many times. And I'd told others the same thing and seen the Lord provide for us over and over. There was certainly no reason to doubt that he would continue to do so. And yet, the uncertainty was like a little gnawing beast inside me. We had no way to get any money, no way to get anything at all besides what we already had on this farm right now. I'd felt so blessed over the fall to be able to can some food for the winter and give to a family in town who had an even more desperate circumstance than we did. But since the weather had turned cold, I'd begun to feel pinched and empty, stretched and afraid.

I couldn't show it. It wasn't right even to feel the way I did. I knew God was faithful. He'd always been faithful. But as Emmie tugged her ear and cried again, I felt a quivering angst. Was I just fooling myself? How could we make the holiday bright for all these kids, in addition to our own? When their own father was the gloomiest one of the bunch? It was too much.

I thought of the Scripture that said to take no thought for what we would eat or drink or what we would have to wear, because God who takes care of the birds would even more provide for us. I was sure that in these depression times there were many across the country who were questioning that. But the words must be true. Somehow.

"We make cookies today?" Berty asked hopefully.

"We'll see. Let me rock Emmie a little and see if I can't get her to nap. Then maybe we'll get started."

Emmie protested, and Berty's squirming didn't help matters a bit. I tried to sing again, just a little, but Rorey interrupted me, her voice suddenly stark and cold.

"It's snowing."

With those words, a thousand crazy worries swirled through my mind. About Samuel on his way to the Posts on foot. And the children soon to be walking home from school. And me here alone with sick children. The first snow of the season, and it had to come today.

It's just flurries, I tried to reassure myself. *Rorey's probably just seeing a few lonely flakes floating down, and maybe that'll be all there is to it. It won't be like last year. No one will get stranded.*

28

No one will be left wondering all night if young Sam Hammond had been able to get through the storm to town and the doctor.

Franky went to the window, and his assessment jarred me. "It's really coming down, Mrs. Wortham."

I heard the fear in Franky's voice and knew that his thoughts were surely not far from mine. But this was silly. This was not last year. Everything would be fine.

"Maybe you'll all be able to go sledding tomorrow," I suggested, hoping I sounded as cheerful and encouraging as I wanted to.

"I don't like snow," Rorey lamented. "I wish it would never snow again."

She was pouty, and it could only be because she was worried too. I knew that she'd liked snow once. Before her mother died, she'd liked sledding, snowmen, and especially snowball fights. But we all seemed shaken off our foundations right now, even though I'd thought we were managing so well.

"Will Mr. Wortham be able t' get to town an' back if this keeps up?" Franky asked, and the simple voicing of such a fear made me feel terribly small.

"Of course," I assured everyone. "It isn't far to the Posts, and they'll help once he gets there."

"I sure hope it quits pretty soon," Franky continued. "I wouldn't want Pa gettin' snowed in over t' home alone."

I stared at him, unable to answer. Somehow I had to draw him from the window, draw his mind, and Rorey's, away from such worries. "Franky, Rorey, do you think you can take a chair over to the closet and pull the Christmas box down for me?"

Franky turned. "The Christmas box? A'ready? Before

Sarah gets home? She likes the Christmas box best of anybody."

"I know. And she'll have plenty of time with what's inside once she gets home. But there's no reason we can't start and give them a little surprise when they get here."

Franky smiled, which made me feel somehow warmer. He went to drag a chair toward the front closet, and Rorey followed him reluctantly. Together they managed to lift the box down from its shelf, carry it across the room in my direction, and then plunk it down on the floor. Berty immediately climbed down from my lap to join them. Even Emmie started squirming and reaching. So I moved to the floor with her, and we all took a look.

There were the little yarn people that the pastor's wife had made with the children last year. Several yards of red and green paper chain. And the big, bright buttons we'd strung on extra yarn and used for ornaments. An egg box full of Emma's precious ornament balls I quickly took from Berty's hands and set behind me. And then I claimed the beautiful little glass nativity set that had been our gift from Pastor and Juanita and rose to put it on the mantel immediately, unwilling to take the chance of it getting broken. Besides those things, there wasn't much more in the box. Only the paper star Rorey and Sarah had made for our tree and the cutout angels and nativity characters the children had drawn to decorate the sitting room wall. We hadn't had any other decorations last year except real greenery cut from the timber, a popcorn garland, and the holiday cookies I hoped to be able to duplicate.

Rorey picked up one of the paper cutout figures, looking

far from enthused. "Are we gonna put up the same paper angels an' stuff?"

"We could. But I think it would be even more fun to make new ones, or at least add some more if you really like these."

"I like dat baby Jesus," Berty informed us.

"I don't," Rorey answered immediately. "Franky made it too big. Bigger even than Mary."

"I was younger then," Franky acknowledged. "I can do better this year."

Rorey frowned at him. "I think somebody else should draw Jesus."

"Okay," he agreed. "You can."

"I don't want to." She pouted again.

I couldn't help wondering if she was still feeling poorly and that was what had her so out of sorts. But Rorey could be difficult on a good day—not always badly behaved but a little hard to work with regardless.

Emmie grabbed for a yarn figure, and I let her have one of the biggest, hoping she wouldn't chew it to bits. But she only clutched it in her fist and snuggled into my shoulder, her little face still damp with tears. I kissed her forehead. Still so warm.

"Franky, will you please bring me Emmie's water?"

I wondered after I asked it why I hadn't called on Rorey to hop up and fetch it for me. She had an easier time getting up and across the house than Franky did with his limp. But Franky was here so often. I was more used to asking things of him. And Rorey wasn't feeling her best today. I thought maybe I ought to coax her back to bed for a while.

Rorey shoved aside the paper cutouts Berty was stacking

in front of her and picked up one of the button ornaments. "What are we gonna do with this other stuff? We ain't got no tree for 'em. Not yet anyhow. Is the pastor comin' over to cut one like last year?"

"No. At least I don't think so. He was just being an extra blessing last year because we were so busy with . . . with everything. I suppose we'll take care of that ourselves this year. Eventually."

"Maybe tomorrow," she said. "Whad'ya think?"

I looked over at her, hoping to see a new spark of enthusiasm for the venture, but she was as straight-faced as ever.

"We can talk to Mr. Wortham about it later," I suggested. "He and Robert, and maybe your big brothers, would love the chore of cutting us a tree."

"Can I cut a twee?" Bert asked.

"Perhaps you can help when the time comes. We'll see."

"Well, whad'ya want this stuff out for now then?" Rorey persisted. "They ain't gonna get the tree right now."

I sighed. "You're right. But I thought we could set out a few things, like the nativity scene on the mantel there, because they look so nice, and to get people in the right mood."

Franky brought Emmie's drink at the same time that Rorey scowled and tossed her button ornament back into the box. "I don't think this stuff gives people a good mood! It just makes us remembery."

"I don't think that's a word," Franky told his sister gently.

"I don't care! An' anyway, how would you know? You're even too dumb for school."

"Rorey, that's enough," I had to scold. "Another cruel word, and you're going back to bed."

"I ain't sick so bad like I was!"

"Then you can manage to behave yourself and apologize to your brother. He is far from dumb."

She apologized begrudgingly, with one quick "sorry," and Franky and Berty looked over all the rest of the paper figures one by one. Berty wanted to know who made every one of them. He didn't remember even the ones he had worked on. But Franky remembered them all.

Rorey'd already had enough of the Christmas box. She got up and headed for the stairs. "Can I play with Sarah's doll?"

"Sure, if you're nice with it."

"I'm always nice with it. Bessie likes me good."

I thought of last year and Sarah's tears after Rorey twice sent the doll tumbling down the steps. But Rorey'd been only six, and dealing with far more than a six-year-old knew how to handle. I took a deep breath as she ran up the stairs to get Sarah's precious Bessie doll. *Surely things will be better this year, heavenly Father. For all of us. Help us.*

"Can I draw dat baby Jesus?" Berty suddenly asked.

"Of course. That's a great idea."

"C'mon, Fwank, let's get paper and C'ayolas." He jerked at his brother, and Franky pulled himself back to his feet and went with Bert to the kitchen for the supplies. *Thank you, Lord, for Bert and Frank*, I prayed. *Maybe with their help I can manage to get everyone feeling Christmasy. Just as you said, "A little child shall lead."*

"I drawed Jesus once before," Berty told me when they

got back to the room. "But this un'll be lots better, ta cut with scissors an' stick on dat wall ober d'ere."

The boys spread out paper and worked together on their drawing.

"Lidda Lor' Jesus," Berty started singing again. "Laid downed his sweet head . . ."

I joined him, singing softly, and moved back to the rocker with Emmie, who was finally sipping at her water again.

"Lidda Lor' Jesus is gots to be the prettiest," Bert told his brother. Their shaggy brown heads bobbed together over the picture.

"You're right," Franky agreed with a quiet voice. "He's the mos' importan' one. We wouldn' have no Christmas without him. And no heaven neither, an' that'd be even worse."

"Really? Dat baby Jesus in heaven?"

"He sure is," Franky answered, as always wise beyond his years. "He made heaven an' ever'thin' in the whole world. E'cept the bad stuff. That's problems the devil throwed in."

"How you know all that?" Berty asked. He, too, was bright. It was plain to see, and I wished their father wouldn't willingly miss out on so many special times with his little ones.

"I jus' listened good," Franky kept on explaining. "T' Mama an' Mrs. Wortham an' the preacher. You can learn a whole lot if you listen good."

"Oh." Berty nodded. "I try that sometime."

I smiled. And Emmie's lidded cup slipped suddenly away from her hand. She rolled against me, her breaths deep and even. So quickly, so peacefully, she was asleep.

"Lidda Lor' Jesus," Berty sang out again. "As'eep on da hay . . ."

The Stars in the Sky

By the time the other children had come home from school, Emmie'd had a nice nap, Rorey's mood had improved a bit, and the boys had helped me hang button ornaments and yarn people from doorknobs and mantel corners, just to be festive. They'd also drawn a new baby Jesus, a wise man, and a tiny little angel.

"This one's little 'cause it's far away," Franky explained. "On the way t' find the shepherds."

But Berty's ear was bothering him again, the snow had increased considerably, and we'd seen nothing at all of Samuel, George, or the doctor.

Sarah was excited to find the Christmas box out on the sitting room floor, but after picking up a pair of paper angels, she grew strangely quiet.

"Come an' play doll with me," Rorey called her.

"Not right now." She stared down at the cutout Crayola drawings. "Do you remember last year we decided that your mama and Emma was our Christmas angels?"

Rorey's face turned red. "See, Franky? See? There is too such a thing as remembery, and Sarah's got it! But we didn't decide nothin'! We didn't! Mama an' Emma jus' died! We didn't tell 'em to go an' be no angels!"

"Stop it," her older brother Kirk told her. "We oughta all just go home."

"Not all of you. Not yet," I said quickly. "Mr. Wortham is getting the doctor for me, to take a look at Emmie."

Kirk frowned. "Pa won't like you callin' the doctor."

"Maybe not," I acknowledged. "But we thought it was best, considering the way she's been feeling. Better not to take any chances."

I was immediately sorry I'd said it that way. Kirk turned his stormy eyes away from me. Joe was looking strangely pale, and Lizbeth took Emmie into her arms. "You think it's bad, Mrs. Wortham?"

"No," I tried to assure everyone. "I just wanted the doctor to advise how to help her be a little more comfortable, that's all. She's had a restless day."

"Me too," Berty announced, even though he'd seemed fine most of the time. "I got a earache."

"Quit complainin'," Willy said. "Nothin' wrong with you 'cept you make too much noise."

"I think I got the earache too," Harry told us, and Lizbeth and I both looked at him in surprise. Harry'd never been sick, not in all the time I'd known him. And as boisterous as he usually was, I would have thought that if he ever did get sick, he probably wouldn't slow down enough to notice.

"Are you sure?" Lizbeth asked him. He did look flushed. And he hadn't chased Bert, though he'd been home all of ten minutes.

"Maybe that's why he was so good in school this afternoon," Joe suggested. "He didn't even get out of his seat once, 'cept when he was supposed to. I wondered then if he was sick. That ain't like Harry at all."

Not another one. I went and felt Harry's forehead, and he was surprisingly warm. Even warmer than Emmie. But maybe he wasn't feeling any worse than Bert. Surely not. Bert had been up and playing most of the day, even after telling me about his ear. He really wasn't sick. And Harry was such an incredibly strong, active little boy. It seemed impossible for him to be so suddenly under the weather.

But he plopped down on the davenport and leaned his head against a cushion. "Teacher said I'm not zippy today," he told me quietly. "I don't think I wanna go tomorrow."

"Maybe you shouldn't," I said with a sigh and glanced over at Lizbeth. She looked like she could burst into tears. "Now, don't worry," I told her quickly. "It's the most normal thing in the world for children to come down with colds and things when the weather gets chill. They'll all be fine. Just look at Rorey. She's feeling much better than she was this morning."

Rorey didn't comment on that at all. She was still put out at Sarah for bringing up her memories, and apparently at the rest of us for failing to pay more attention.

"I don't want the Christmas stuff out," she complained. "Put it away."

"Oh, Rorey, I know it's hard," I tried to sympathize.

"No, you don't! You let Mama go away! You let her go all the way to heaven—"

"Rorey Jeanine," Lizbeth warned. "You know as well as anybody that it weren't Mrs. Wortham's fault."

Something shook inside me. I could picture Wila on her bed, Emma in that rocker, both of them fading, with nothing I could do.

"You apologize," Lizbeth scolded her sister. "It's plain foolish to be pointin' blame. Mrs. Wortham's been a godsend to us, and you well know it."

Rorey didn't apologize. Kirk looked my way with a purposed frown. "You oughta keep most of the kids over here, I guess. But Pa was sore from fallin' this mornin', so at least one a' us oughta go and see t' evening chores."

"I'll go," Joe volunteered. "I wanted t' check on Pa anyway." He put his hand on Harry's forehead for a moment. "You rest, trooper," he said. "Behave yourself." He looked over at Rorey. "You too."

"I'm comin' with you," Kirk told him, and I encouraged them both to bundle up carefully. I really couldn't argue with them wanting to go home long enough to see to the necessary farm chores. They were just being diligent and helpful the way boys their age ought to be. But I didn't like them going, I couldn't say why. I just felt uncomfortable with them heading out again in the snow, even though it had lessened and it really wasn't terribly blustery or cold. Nothing like some of the awful storms last winter.

If Samuel had already gotten there, it was probably

unnecessary for them to go. Samuel would help George with the chores before coming back home to meet the doctor here. But I couldn't be sure.

"Hopefully Mr. Wortham's been by to tell your father about the doctor coming, but if not, you let him know. And tell him I've got a pot of soup on the stove that's been simmering most of the day," I told the boys. "I'm going to add dumplings. And he's welcome to join us. I'd like for him to."

"Yes, ma'am," Joe said. "But I doubt he'll come."

Surely he will, I told myself. These are his kids! He ought to come, even if it's just to talk to the doctor and then take them all back home.

Robert and Willy went out to tend to chores here while Joe and Kirk started toward their farm. I got Sarah and Katie started drawing angels and shepherds. True to her word earlier, Rorey only watched. With a far-off look in his eye, Franky held a piece of paper rolled in his hand, and I figured he was concentrating on what to draw next. Lizbeth held Emmie on her lap, playing quietly with a couple of the yarn figures. Harry was soon asleep on the davenport, which was so startling that I was glad to have called for the doctor. Harry was usually wilder than a stampede of horses after being cooped up all day at school. Berty, who usually joined him in his ruckuses, didn't seem to know what to do. He followed me into the kitchen, looking rather forlorn.

"Now Harry's sick too," he said with a sigh.

"I suppose so, but I don't think it's bad with any of you. How's your ear?"

"Still hurts."

"But you seem to be feeling fine otherwise."

He shook his head. "My tummy feels jumbly. And my insides is sad 'bout Harry."

I took him in my arms for a little squeeze. "Harry'll be fine. He just needs to rest after school today."

"He usually needs t' let his legs run loose."

Despite his peculiar way of putting that, I nodded. "I know. But he'll be fine. Let him sleep."

I wondered what Berty meant by his tummy feeling "jumbly," but I didn't ask him. I really didn't want him dwelling too much on such things. I figured whatever it was would pass, and he'd be back to himself pretty much like he'd been all day.

"What're you gonna do?" he asked me.

"Make dumplings like I told your brothers."

"I like dumplin's."

"Good. I know your older brothers do too. I'll have to make plenty."

"Pa likes dumplin's."

I glanced over at him and was not surprised to see his usually bright eyes looking sad. Maybe even at his young age he could sense a struggle in his father the way I did. I prayed that George would come and join us for this meal. I prayed that he was feeling all right. With several of his children seeming to come down with something, maybe he was a bit under the weather too.

"Can I help?" Berty asked, and I obliged him, though there really wasn't much he could do.

He soon lost interest and left me alone. I assumed he'd gone off to play, or joined the girls in the other room to draw Christmas angels. But it wasn't two minutes before I heard a strange clunk behind me.

Berty had a chair tipped on its side on the floor. "Do you need help setting that back up?" I asked him, thinking he'd bumped it over accidentally.

"Nope. Can I make a cow barn?"

"What?"

"With room for sheep an' chickens an' baby Jesus too."

He tipped another chair, and I just stood there with my mixing spoon in hand, not sure what to tell him. He ducked under the table.

"Looky! This is jus' right." He pulled at one of the fallen chairs. "This can be the trough where we're gonna put the baby. An' I'm Joseph, 'cause I'm big."

I smiled. "It's all right to play under the table until time to eat. Then the chairs will all have to stand up again."

Looking like he had serious business to accomplish, he pulled another chair over and moved it against the table legs to form a wall. Then apparently deciding that this game was too good to keep to himself, he went running into the sitting room, hollering with excitement.

"Sarah! Sarah! Can your dolly be Jesus? An' you can be Mary! Or Rorey or Katie can! Or else angels! Franky! Come an' be a shepherd!"

I didn't try to shush him so he wouldn't disturb Harry or get Emmie worked up. I wasn't about to squelch his exuberance. I'd prayed for God to be with us and help us this Christmas. And he'd sure sunk Christmas deep into Berty's heart. That was all the boy had wanted to think about all day.

But not Rorey. She was holding Sarah's doll, and she did not want to give it up for Berty's manger. And Franky's perfect solution that Rorey pretend to be Mary did not sit well

41

with her at all. "I don't wanna play that! I wanna be a modern mommy! And we's in a house, not some old manger."

"I'll be Mary," Sarah volunteered sweetly. "We can pretend the baby isn't borned yet."

"But I want you to play with me," Rorey immediately protested.

"I can play with you," little Katie offered.

"No! I don't want you!"

Rorey had never welcomed Katie's arrival on the scene. She seemed to see the younger girl as nothing more than a distraction when what she wanted was Sarah's undivided attention. But I couldn't simply ignore her rude words. Katie had been brave even to offer. I left my bowl of dumpling batter in the kitchen and followed the voices into the sitting room.

"Rorey, please come here a moment."

She stuck out her lip. "Are you gonna make me play Mary?"

"No. Absolutely not. But I do want to talk to you."

She threw the doll down on the floor and stomped her little feet in my direction.

"Honey, Katie was being very nice to offer to play with you. You shouldn't be so unkind to her."

"But I don't wanna play with that girl."

"Fine. She can play with Sarah and Berty. She'd make a lovely angel or shepherd girl. You can come and sit in a chair beside me in the kitchen."

"There ain't no shepherd girls," Rorey whined. "There's only shepherd boys. An' anyway, that girl oughta go away! She don't b'long here with this fam'ly all the time. Her mama ain't dead."

"Rorey Jeanine!" Lizbeth scolded immediately.

And I was about to say something too, but the look on Katie's face stopped me cold. She tried, she tried very hard, but there was no way to hold it back. The poor child burst into tears.

"Go sit in a chair, Rorey," Lizbeth commanded. "Right this minute."

Rorey stormed into the kitchen and Lizbeth followed her, taking Emmie along. I let them be and took Katie into my arms.

"Boy," Sarah observed. "Rorey sure is mean when she don't feel good."

Katie clung to me, and I held her tight. I'd thought Rorey was feeling better, but even if she wasn't, there was no excuse for such an outburst, especially at another child's expense. I put my hand on Katie's hair, but she wouldn't raise her head enough for me to see her face. "Sweetie, she was just talking mean. You do belong with us. You're family, and we love you."

Sarah reached for the little girl's hand. "I don't want Katie to go away. I like her here."

"So do I."

Katie didn't even seem to hear us. She'd buried her face into my shoulder and wept as though her heart had been broken. I felt like thrashing Rorey good, but I could hear Lizbeth scolding her in the kitchen, and it wasn't long before Rorey was crying too. Robert and Willy came in from doing chores and glanced about at all the long faces.

"Man, is ever'body gettin' sick?" Willy shook his head and threw a log on the fire. "Pa ain't gonna like this one bit."

"Mom," Robert said somberly. "It's thunderin'. You ever hear that before with snow?"

I hadn't heard anything, but it wasn't any wonder with all the commotion inside. "I think so. I'm just not sure right now when it was."

"When's Dad supposed to be here with the doctor? When did he leave?"

"Shortly after lunch." I knew Robert was thinking way too hard about how much time it should have taken him, which I had not allowed myself to do.

"That's plenty of time to get to town an' back," he told me with a troubled frown.

"He started off walking," I explained. "And even if he got the use of the Posts' truck, he might be driving more slowly than usual to see through the falling snow."

"Mom—"

"He'll be here any minute," I spoke positively. "He won't let himself be delayed."

Robert didn't answer. He just moved to the fire and added a log right on top of the one Willy had just thrown in. Rorey was still crying in the kitchen. Katie still clung to me, and I could hear Emmie fussing now too.

"It'll be dark 'fore long," Willy said glumly.

I ignored the implications, the worry, in those words. "I'll light the lamps and finish the dumplings," I told him cheerfully. "Robert, it would sure be nice if you could try to find us some pretty music to listen to on the radio. Hopefully it'll work tonight."

Berty was ready to go right back to playing manger scene, and Sarah helped to still Katie's tears by asking her to please come and be an angel. Hand in hand they followed Berty under the table as Robert struggled to get any reception from our beat-up old radio. Finally we heard a few instrumental strains of "God Rest Ye Merry, Gentlemen," but then he turned it off because it got too staticky to hear whatever played next. It didn't matter. By then, Berty was singing again to beat the band. Rorey was still pouting, but at least she was quieter. And Harry, incredibly, slept through everything.

I could tell Lizbeth was concerned about Harry and about Emmie's continuing fever. Berty seemed fine, but with Rorey it was difficult to tell. She sat. She sulked. She didn't complain that she was feeling poorly. But she did complain about just about everything else. "Don't want dumplin's for supper," she grouched at me. "Don't want no soup neither."

"Aren't you getting hungry?"

"Nope."

"You might want just a little bit, when the time comes."

"Uh-uh."

"Well, that's all right. I'm not going to make anybody eat who isn't hungry."

I put the dumplings in the pot, praying that Samuel would be back soon. Robert and Willy were starting a game of checkers, but that didn't mean they were thinking any less. Rorey started fidgeting in the chair, but Lizbeth wouldn't let her get up. She complained bitterly about the other children using Sarah's doll now, but Lizbeth would not let her have it back because she'd behaved so badly to Katie and then thrown the doll on the floor.

"You can just stay where you are till you wise up and apologize," Lizbeth told her.

But Rorey was in too stubborn of a mood today for that. She sat in the only upright kitchen chair with her arms crossed, her legs swinging, and her lip poked out far enough for a bird to land on it. And all the while, Berty went right on playing Joseph under the table as though she weren't even there. He seemed so perky that it took me absolutely by surprise when he suddenly leaned against one of the tipped-over chairs and threw up almost in the exact spot where Rorey'd been sick this morning. She turned absolutely green at the sight and looked like she might lose it again too.

"Oh no," I said, grabbing the nearest dishtowel.

"Sorry, sorry," Berty told me, backing up a couple of steps and then plopping to the floor.

What next? I dismissed Rorey from her chair so she could get out of sight of the mess, and she hurried from the kitchen only to come very close to losing the remains of her lunch in the sitting room.

"I think we have what Teacher calls the stomach bug around here," Sarah told me.

"And an ear bug and a fever bug too," I added. "But maybe it's all part of the same thing."

"That's a bad bug," Katie said quietly.

"I wouldn't argue with that," I answered her and cleaned up the mess the best I could. I was beginning to wonder who'd be able to eat around here, and whether this illness, whatever it was, would try to make its way through the rest of the kids. At least it hadn't hit any of them too awfully hard. Franky had gotten so quiet I was beginning to wonder about him. He dipped a bowl of water to rinse my dishtowel and looked at me with such a serious expression.

"Mrs. Wortham, don't ya think we need manger people that ain't flat?"

That question had certainly come out of the blue. "What?"

"Like the perty manger scene at our church, or the glass one you put on the mantel outta reach. The flat paper ones is good for stickin' on the wall, but don't you think we need some to stand up like they's supposed to—I mean, that it's okay for kids to touch? They sure would look nice sittin' on the table."

"Um . . ." I wasn't sure I could give that a lot of thought right now. A stand-up manger scene? A nice idea, of course, but with supper cooking and several sick kids . . .

"I gots it worked out," he announced. "Wanna see?"

I finished wiping the floor and grasped a table leg to help pull myself off my knees. "Uh, all right."

He ran to where the paper and Crayolas had been abandoned on the sitting room floor and came limping back to me with his rolled-up paper in his hand. "We can make a cone—see? That'd stand up real good. Then we can roll a little piece of paper and stick it right on top for a head and put hair or a shepherd's hat or something on it. An' we can color in the faces and the clothes an' stuff. I ain't got it all figgered how to make the manger that baby Jesus is layin' in, but I think I can do it. I'd like to carve ever'thin' outta wood someday for ya, but ever'body can help with this'un outta paper for this year."

"That's a very nice idea, Franky," I told him, even though I wasn't really sure it would work very well. I could just see Harry, or Emmie, or Bert carelessly squashing beyond repair any stand-up paper figures left within reach.

47

Bert had ducked back under the table and was eyeing me carefully. "That was a icky mess."

"Yes, but you couldn't help it. How are you feeling now? Do you need to lie down a little while?"

He shook his head. "I'm not sick no more. I think I cans get back t' playin'."

I wasn't sure he'd ever stopped. Apparently he had a pretty strong constitution about him. Rorey, however, had gone back to my bed, and Harry was still conked out on the couch.

Berty linked arms with Sarah, and Katie majestically handed the "baby Jesus" Bessie doll under the table to them. I wondered for a moment if the girls ought to be playing so closely with him, but I figured that if there was anything to be caught, it would already be too late now, and there was no sense spoiling their fun. I moved to the stove to check my dumpling pot. Franky followed right behind me.

"Can we try them stand-up people?"

"Yes. I suppose so. But not right now. I—"

A sound outside stopped me. A vehicle on our drive. Thank the Lord! It must be Samuel with the doctor, or with George. Or both.

"Hallelujah!" I proclaimed. "I think that's Samuel coming home."

Frank gave a knowing nod. "Sure hope he brung the doctor. Some folks is kinda sick 'round here."

In less than two shakes, we heard Samuel's footsteps on the porch. I was thrilled he was finally home. But unfortunately, he was alone.

"The doctor'll be here in a few minutes," Samuel told

48

me first thing as he came through the door. "Barrett asked that he stop at their house first since Louise is doing so much worse and it didn't sound as if Emmie were too serious. I hope I did the right thing agreeing, but Barrett's pretty worried about his wife today. He was glad I came by and mentioned the doctor. He wanted to go, but he didn't want to leave her."

"It's all right," I told him and gave him a big hug. "Just knowing the doctor's on the way is a blessed relief. Emmie's no worse, but she's not the only one I want him to look at now. I pray Louise is all right."

"Rorey feeling poorly again?" he asked me, looking around a little.

"And Harry. And Bert."

Bert and the girls were still playing under the table. Samuel glanced their way and gave me a quizzical look. "Bert looks fine."

"I'm glad he does, but he was sick to his stomach not ten minutes ago. It won't hurt to have the doctor take a look, since he'll be here anyway."

"And Harry? Where's he?"

"He laid down right after school and hasn't got up since. He was fevering and complaining of earache."

Samuel knew Harry as well as I did. "Maybe he's the one the doctor ought to look at first when he gets over here. It's not like Harry to want to lie down. Even at bedtime."

"I know."

Samuel gave me another hug and kissed the top of my head.

"Where's George?" I asked him. "Didn't he want to come with you?"

He looked over at the children again and took my hand. "Come here a minute, Julia. I've got something I need to show you." He reached for my coat on the hook beside the back door. Lizbeth was just coming back to the kitchen from the other room.

"Rorey wants me to get her a glass of water," she told us. "I'm sorry the way she behaved, but I think she's feverin' again. She's just not herself."

"It's all right," I told her. "I'll be right back in."

Lizbeth looked at us oddly as I pulled on my coat. But there was no way I could explain, and Samuel didn't even try. I knew he had something to tell me that he didn't want the children to hear, and that understanding was sitting sour in my stomach. *Not more to bear, Lord. What could be wrong?*

Samuel drew me close at the porch edge, and we looked out over our newly snowy yard. The breeze was cold, but there was nothing but flurries coming down now, like tiny stinging wet kisses.

"I didn't find George," he told me, holding me tight. "The house was empty. No sign of him. I met the boys over there doing chores. I offered to give them a ride back to get some supper, but they said they might wait awhile and see if he comes back. He didn't take a horse, but Joe checked the house and said he did take what money was saved back in a fruit jar."

"Oh, Samuel."

"There's no reason to think he won't be back tonight."

"But he could be drunk and wild as anything! How much money did they have?"

"I don't know, but it wasn't much. And I thought it

was going toward Christmas. He told me last week that since we'd be feeding them all, he was going to go to town and get a box of groceries to bring with them Christmas Eve."

"Well, maybe . . . maybe he went to town today for that."

He shook his head. "Not without the horse and wagon. Not without telling anybody. He's gone off on foot, and I think he wanted the little ones with you today, sick or not, so he could do this."

My heart was pounding, thinking about Lizbeth and the big boys. George left so much on them all the time. And on us. And now this. "What if he's not back tonight?"

Samuel's sigh was deep and pained. "You know how he was last year, Juli. I'm just hoping. But I don't think I can wait and do nothing. He's not on their farm. I checked best I could. I needed to talk to you so you wouldn't wonder what was keeping me, but I think I should go and see if Buck Fraley's seen him. There's a few places I could check."

I nodded. George was a grown man. We could just let it go. Wait. Surely he'd come back in good time. But he'd been out of his mind in his grief last year. Forgetful of the children and everything else. Suicidal. And I knew Samuel was right. Even though a year had passed and George had been his normal self most of that time, we couldn't be sure what shape he was in tonight.

"You should send those boys back over here, Samuel. Maybe it's better that they not be home if their father comes in drunk—"

"I'll stop and tell them to come for supper. Are you doing

all right here, Juli, with several kids sick? I hate to leave you, not knowing how long I'll be."

"The doctor's on his way. Lizbeth's here. And Robert and Willy are old enough to be a big help if I need them."

He kissed me. "All right. I'll be back as soon as I can."

He left in Mr. Post's truck. Without eating a bite. What would we do if George just disappeared into the night, leaving ten kids without their father? How would they feel, how would they react? Surely George would think about their needs! I prayed that he was already.

I knew it wouldn't be long before the children started asking questions. Probably Lizbeth or Franky first, since their father hadn't come and Samuel had left again so quickly. What could I tell them? That he just went off, who knew where?

If it'd been any other man I knew, it wouldn't have been a cause for worry, and I would feel silly for even dwelling on it. George could be helping a neighbor, looking for livestock that had gotten out, or working on a Christmas surprise for his family. It could be any number of things. But George was different. He had a hard time with liquor and an even harder time holding himself together if he got to thinking too much about the mother of his children. He'd done fairly well in the past year, considering the kind of father he'd been before Wila died. But he fell apart far too easily. Samuel and I'd had no idea we would become so tied to the lives of our neighbor children. But what else could we do?

I stood there looking out over the farmyard in the cold, trying to find words to pray. I knew I needed to get back inside. Probably all the children were wondering by now what in the world we were up to. They might worry, if they'd heard Samuel driving off. But I hesitated, feeling ill-equipped to face the questions of the precious children waiting in my house for the doctor, their father, and some good reason to celebrate this Christmas.

What could I tell them? I knew deep down that George's disappearance was not some innocent little jaunt. How could he do this? He'd promised us, he'd promised his children, that he would leave the booze alone and do his best.

The evening had grown so still. The breeze died back, and the flurries had slowed to a stop. Glancing up at the dark above me, I expected to see only the dusky swirl of clouds. But to the south, the sky was different. Just a piece of it opened up, just a whisper, a tiny window into the field of stars beyond the clouds. And the glimpse seemed like a promise, a tiny glimmer of hope. With a prayer in my heart, I turned and went back inside.

Asleep on the Hay

*J*ust as I expected, Lizbeth asked about her father almost as soon as I got back inside. I didn't want to tell her he wasn't home, but Joe and Kirk already knew and they'd surely tell her when they got back, so there was little point in trying to keep it from her.

"He's gone out for a bit," I told her simply. "Mr. Wortham hasn't spoken to him yet."

"Out where? Did he take a horse?"

"No, he didn't. But he didn't seem to be on your farm."

I saw her face change, her thoughts darkening, just as mine had. But Franky was standing close by, so she didn't voice anything negative. "Well, if he went walkin', his back must be feeling better."

"Where would he go?" Franky questioned. "If he was headed to town, he'd a' took the wagon."

"Not necessarily," Lizbeth answered vaguely. "'Sides, he mighta gone somewhere besides town. Maybe he's just talkin' to God and Mama in the timber."

Frank looked a little doubtful, but he didn't argue. "If that's it, he'll be back perty soon." The words came out lightly enough, but I knew the gravity in Franky's unusual silvery gray eyes. Neither he nor his sister said any more about it, though. Harry was stirring, and Franky went to keep Berty from jumping on him. Lizbeth got Emmie a cup of the fresh milk Robert had brought in. I put my arm around her shoulders for a brief little squeeze, and she whispered, "Thank you, Mrs. Wortham."

We ate soup with dumplings for an early supper. Without Samuel, and without George. Joe and Kirk were back in time to join us, but the doctor still hadn't arrived. I said a prayer for Louise Post along with the grace for our meal, hoping there wasn't something serious going on. We were a dreadfully dreary group crowded around the supper table. Rorey and Harry both joined us but didn't eat very much. Berty didn't want anything at all, which was probably for the best at the moment. Emmie had nothing but milk, and only a little of that. It was Willy who was the most full of questions.

"Why didn't Pa wanna come over?"

"He ain't home," Kirk answered before I had a chance to phrase things more gently.

"Where'd he go?"

Lizbeth looked at me, but once again Kirk answered before I got the chance. "Who knows? He just ain't home."

"Maybe he wanted t' buy us somethin'," Harry suggested.

"Yeah, right," Kirk scoffed.

"You don't know nothin'," Joe told him. "It's possible. You know he always buys us candy in December."

"He'd a' took the horse and wagon if he was goin' to town," Kirk echoed Franky's understanding.

"It don't take no wagon to haul home Christmas candy," Joe argued. He forced a little smile. "He didn't have money for that much."

"Well, he's a grown man," I told everyone. "And since it is December, it's probably best not to keep up our guessing." I knew the skepticism in the children's faces, especially Willy and Kirk. But I deeply appreciated Joe's optimism. Far better for the little ones to have a little ordinary hopefulness than a fearful doubting of their father's intentions. None of us really knew. Joe might be right, as unlikely as it sounded. And what a relief that would be.

Unfortunately, the uncertainty left everybody a little testy and glum. Nobody really believed that George had walked eight miles on a snowy day to do holiday shopping.

Rorey came very close to losing the little bit she'd eaten. Harry went back to the davenport to lie down before we'd even started clearing the dishes. When I went to check on him, he felt so warm I decided to bathe his forehead with a cool cloth. I'd never seen Harry like this, and I wished the doctor could find a way to hurry.

Emmie seemed a little better despite her lack of appetite. She still pulled at one ear, but she wasn't as fussy now, and she seemed content to sit with Joe on the floor and play a little more with the yarn dolls.

Lizbeth, along with Sarah, helped me clean up. Katie started in too, but then she quietly just left us and went upstairs. That seemed a little strange for her, and I was about to go up to the girls' room and see if she was all right, when finally I heard another vehicle outside. Not Samuel this time. It was a car, and not as loud as Mr. Post's truck.

I was so glad to see old Dr. Howell. He came slowly up our porch steps, and I flung the door open before he even got to it.

"How's that baby?" he asked me as he stepped in.

"Doing better, but there are three other—"

Before I could finish what I was saying, Berty ran up and tugged the doctor's coat sleeve. "I got a earache. I throwed up too. But Harry—he's sicker'n me. He ain't even played at all today!"

"Well, sounds like I need to take a look at that boy. Were you saying there are three sick now, Mrs. Wortham?"

"In addition to the baby. But I do think you should look at Harry first."

I took his coat and draped it over a chair back because our coat hooks were full of the Hammond children's wraps and things. Everybody watched as I led the doctor to Harry's side. He looked in his throat and ears and took his temperature, asking only a few questions. Then he wanted to see Emmie. Then Rorey, and then Bert, who'd been standing at his elbow and chattering impatiently the whole time.

"These four are all Hammonds, aren't they?" the doctor asked, looking around at the other children's faces.

"Yes," I answered, not really sure why he'd asked.

"Is their father here?"

57

The room was suddenly stark still. "No, sir."

"Are they staying the night with you, then?"

"I expect so."

"Good. Gonna be awful cold, I heard. They've got no business being in the night air. Keep them home from school tomorrow. Every one of them. Yours too, Mrs. Wortham, even the ones who are feeling fine today. You've got a touch of the stomach flu plus ear infections in the youngest three. Might not spread to the rest, but there's no sense taking chances on it going through the whole school. Everybody else feeling all right?"

Twelve children in the house. Maybe it was a wonder only the youngest Hammonds had been affected. But then I remembered Katie.

"Um, Doctor, excuse me. Somebody's missing." I hurried upstairs, leaving the doctor with a roomful of children and praying that Katie wasn't feeling sick as well.

I didn't see her at first when I got to the girls' room. I had to step in and around the corner of the bed before I found her on the floor, all curled up and in tears.

"Oh, Katie. What's wrong? Are you feeling bad?"

I put my hand on her forehead, but she didn't feel warm.

"Jus' my heart," she said in a voice so quiet I barely heard her.

I sat down. "What's wrong?"

She hesitated, her dark eyes brimming with tears. But apparently she decided it was best to tell me what she could. "I been dreamin' about Mommy."

She looked so awfully forlorn that I couldn't help but pull her into my arms. "Last night?"

She nodded.

"Honey, I know you miss her. And it surely didn't help, the mean things Rorey said earlier."

"Rorey's just sad," Katie tried to explain. "And I think mad too, 'cause my mommy's still alive."

"Yes. But that doesn't make it easy for you, that she's not here with you. And I wish I could do something about that—"

Katie shook her head. Adamantly. "No."

"Maybe your grandmother has been able to find out where she is."

"No." She shook her head again. And then she burst into fresh tears.

"Katie, I'm not sure what you're telling me. Are you afraid your grandma won't find her?"

"No."

She could barely answer me. She'd cried a lot when she first came to us, but it had been months since I'd seen any tears, and even then it wasn't like this. "Are you sure you're feeling all right? The doctor's still here, and we should go down—"

"No. I . . . I dreamed Mommy came back—"

"I still believe she will. One day. She just doesn't seem to understand what she's missing, not spending time with her wonderful little girl—"

"No"—she squeezed at me—"I . . . I don't want her to take me away."

I was speechless for a moment, realizing I might have had things backward.

She was shaking her head. "I wanna stay with you."

"Honey, you will. We don't even know where she is. But don't you miss her?"

This time, she nodded, struggling to speak. "Sometimes I want Mommy. I wish she'd come and see me. But . . . but sometimes I wish she was dead like Rorey's mommy."

"Oh, honey."

"I feel mixed up and bad inside."

"Confused, I think. That's what you mean. And I understand, sweetie. I know you love her. But it wasn't easy when you were with her. She needs our prayers. I'm sure she loves you. She just didn't know how to show it."

Katie's mother had never been attentive to her needs and had finally abandoned her, just leaving her with Samuel's brother Edward, a man she barely knew, to run off and pursue a singing career in honky-tonks and clubs. I still could scarcely fathom a mother doing that. And it made my stomach tighten just thinking about the day Edward had shown up here with Katie hidden in his car. Terrible, rough-shod Edward with his awful accusations.

"Is Rorey's pa gonna go away like my mommy?" Katie asked then. "Maybe Rorey wouldn't care, but there's all them. Lots of kids. Is they gonna be sad and confused like me?"

I held her tight for a moment before I could answer. "Maybe they already are. In a way. Grieving their mother. And their father needs our prayers too. He just doesn't seem to know how to handle things . . ."

I knew I shouldn't be telling a six-year-old much of anything about George. And yet she seemed to understand something of my worries. "Honey, we should go downstairs. The doctor is surely wondering."

She looked up at me. "Does he know anything about heart hurts?"

I took a deep breath. "I'm sure he does. But unfortunately, there's not much he can do about things like that."

"Then I don't need to see him."

I brushed a few dark curls away from her eyes. "I guess not. But I need to talk to him about what we can do to get Harry and Emmie and the others feeling better. Do you want to come with me?"

She took my hand. I started to get up, but she didn't move. "If Mommy does come back, are you gonna send me away with her?"

"It's not quite so simple," I admitted. "Because . . . because of her leaving you the way she did before, Samuel and I have become your guardians. We couldn't just send you away now unless we knew it was best. Do you understand?"

She nodded. "Mommy'd just go away without me again, to go and sing someplace else."

"Yes. Unless she's changed an awful lot, she probably would. But it's not all right, you know that, just to go off and leave your child."

"Uncle Eddie scared me."

For a moment, I couldn't answer. Samuel's brother had stirred anger in me like I'd never felt for anyone. And fear. Not just of his unpredictable temper, but of what he was trying to do to my husband, coming here and accusing him of being Katie's father. I knew it wasn't true. Samuel had never even met Katie's mother. It had all been a strange misunderstanding, and we'd learned that Katie was probably their sister. But Edward had come with such a chip on his shoulder, such a vindictive desire to hurt his brother. He'd even come to blows. None of us would soon forget, despite the change of heart before he left.

"I know he scared you," I managed to tell her. "He scared me too. I'm glad now that he brought you to us, but that doesn't make it right the way things happened, and what your mother did."

She lowered her eyes. "I hope Rorey's pa just went to the store."

I smiled a little and took a deep breath to calm the churning inside me. "I hope so too." I helped her to her feet, and she came with me down the stairs to join everyone else. I let the doctor look her over, but he didn't find anything wrong. I guess I knew he wouldn't. He seemed to know our situation. At least he understood that Katie wasn't a Hammond, or my own daughter either.

"I'd say it's more than stomach flu ailing the whole lot here," Dr. Howell told me privately. "You do remarkably well, Mrs. Wortham, but it's a wonder things aren't worse. So close to Christmas, and so many children without a mother. You make sure and take extra good care of yourself along with these young ones. Seems like you're going to be spread awfully thin."

I couldn't find any way to answer that. He gave me quinine for the fevers, Oltman's Stomach Remedy to help any nausea, and wintergreen oil for Harry, Berty, and Emmie's ears. A generous supply of all three, in case any of the other children got to feeling poorly.

"Keep them in bed all you can," he admonished. "Though

I realize it won't be easy with that youngest boy. At least try to keep him restful."

"We can't pay you today—" I started to explain.

He waved his hand like he was dismissing the idea. "Talk to George about it when you get the chance. He can bring me some eggs or a bit of bacon one of these days."

"Thank you."

"Merry Christmas," he said. "I hope you don't need me again before then."

"How's Mrs. Post?"

"The poor woman's had an awful struggle with the influenza. Looks to be a touch of pneumony on top of that. It's got her down weak. Keep her in your prayers. She may still be in bed for Christmas, but I believe she'll recover."

I nodded. The Posts had been such good neighbors to us, and to the Hammonds, and now to have such troubles! No wonder Barrett had been worried. I tried to consider whether there was anything we could do for them.

But I didn't have time to think about that long. Berty was pulling at my sleeve.

"Joe says I'm gonna hafta rest. Does 'at mean right now?"

"You at least need to be doing quiet things, the doctor said. And it won't be long before time to settle everyone down for bed."

It was still early, but I knew I'd better set things in motion now. It always took a little planning to bed down so many Hammonds at our house.

"You want us to bring the mattresses down, Mom?" Robert asked me.

We'd done that before, putting the bed mattresses on

the floor for some and letting others sleep on quilt-covered box springs, to put something besides floor under most of us on a chilly night. "That'd be fine," I told him. "But just slide the one in your room onto the floor and leave it there. I think I'll let you big boys all stay upstairs."

Robert, Willy, and Joe all headed up to move the mattresses. I expected Kirk to go with them, but he just stood at the base of the stairs and stared at me. "Why do we need to stay here? We come back over for supper 'cause Mr. Wortham told us to, but why shouldn't we go home?"

My insides felt pinched a little just seeing the fiery look in his eyes. "The doctor said the little ones have no business being out in the night air tonight."

"I ain't talkin' 'bout the little ones."

"Kirk," Lizbeth interjected. "Don't you think it's better to be together?"

"Why? What if Pa comes home? He'd 'spect us to be home, wouldn't he?"

"No," I told him soberly. "I think he would expect you to be here. I think he planned it that way and is probably counting on it. He knows that Lizbeth and I would not be comfortable with the little ones over there sick tonight without a parent."

"I said I'm not talkin' 'bout the little ones! We ain't all little, you—"

"Kirk!" Lizbeth cut him off. "You hold your tongue and go help with the mattresses. This minute."

Lizbeth had been the boss since they'd lost their mother. I'd seldom seen any of the others question their big sister, let alone exhibit any real defiance. But tonight, Kirk was different.

64

"I don't hafta do what you say. An' I don't hafta do what Mrs. Wortham says! You ain't Mama or Pa, and if I ain't got neither a' them no more, I can decide stuff for myself! I don't need you tellin' me—"

"You think you're grown up, do you, Kirk Thomas?" Lizbeth fumed. "You're not but thirteen, and you still got a pa! And me! And you're not gonna act otherwise. Now get up there an' help!"

Beside me, Katie shook a little. I knew she hated yelling. She hated arguing. And Bert and Emmie were both staring at us, taking in the commotion.

"Kirk," I said quietly, hoping to calm things a little. "It's all right to want to go home. I understand that. But please wait till Mr. Wortham gets here. Even as big as you are, I hate the thought of you heading out through the timber again alone tonight."

"There ain't nothin' out there but cold," he scoffed.

"The cold is bad enough," I said. "So is the aloneness."

"Maybe Joe or Willy'd go with me," he offered.

"Willy likes to stay with Robert," Lizbeth said more calmly. "An' I could use Joe's help here if any of the younger ones is sick in the night."

"You ain't gotta wait at home for Pa," Franky suddenly said from across the room. "He knows t' find us here if he wants. But he won't look tonight."

"What d'you know?" Kirk scoffed.

"I know he tol' us 'fore we lef' this morning to mind Mrs. Wortham good."

"He always means for us to do that," Kirk continued his argument.

"But he don't always say it."

Kirk and Lizbeth both stared at Franky. But Rorey was the one to speak up. "That don't mean nothin'! Not nothin' at all!"

"Hush," Lizbeth told her and turned her attention immediately back to Frank. "I was busy with Emmie this morning. Did he say anythin' else?"

Franky shook his head. "I jus' thought a' that. Jus' now."

"It don't mean nothin'," Kirk echoed Rorey's words. "He jus' knowed we was stoppin' here 'fore school like always, that's all."

Franky didn't say a word. He didn't have to. The coldness of the idea that their father may have planned to leave settled over me as well as over Kirk and Lizbeth. But Berty just didn't understand.

"Pa gonna sleep here tonight too?" he asked his big sister. "We gonna make him a bed?"

"If he comes with Mr. Wortham," I said quickly before Lizbeth had a chance to answer. "We can fix him a bed when he gets here."

Lizbeth looked at me in question.

"Who's gonna do chores over t' home in the mornin'?" Kirk suddenly asked.

"Any of you boys could go," I said. "Once it's daylight, all right?"

"Please, Kirk," Lizbeth added. "Let's stay together tonight. I don't wanna be wonderin' 'bout you too."

"I wouldn't go nowhere but home," he said softly.

"I know. But the doctor kinda wanted us all to stay in anyhow, 'case any of the rest of us was to catch somethin'. Remember? Even tomorrow."

Joe and Robert were maneuvering down the stairs with Katie and Sarah's mattress. Willy followed with one of the blankets that had been on top.

"You should pull the mattress off our bed too," I told the boys. "That way I think we can keep everybody off the wood floor."

Without a word, Kirk headed into the bedroom for the mattress. There was no more talk of anyone leaving that night.

I pulled out all of the spare sheets and blankets we had and got all the bedding situated for everybody. Of course, the beds wouldn't be quite so comfortable tonight without the top mattresses, but we'd all make do. Katie and Sarah on their bed, Willy and Robert on his. And Samuel with me, when he got home. I'd put Kirk and Franky on the mattress in Robert's room and Harry and Berty on one down here. Rorey really wanted to sleep in Sarah's room, but Lizbeth thought she ought to stay downstairs with her and Emmie on the other mattress since she'd been sick too. I fixed a bed for Joe on the davenport where he'd be close if Lizbeth needed him like she'd suggested.

"Do we hafta go to bed a'ready?" Rorey asked me, and I was a little surprised that she didn't want to, but I guess I shouldn't have been, considering the nap she took.

It seemed late. It seemed like half the night had progressed, but one look at the mantel clock told me that it really wasn't late at all. Time never seemed to flow the same when Samuel was gone in the evening. I tried not to worry about what he might have found, or not found, but it was hard to keep such things out of my thoughts. And I wasn't the only one. A sleepover with neighbors ought to be fun, at least a little bit, even if some of the kids were feeling a little under the weather. But nobody looked very happy, even though the youngest seemed to feel a little better after their first dose of the medicine Dr. Howell had left.

I knew Emmie was tired. But Lizbeth didn't try to settle her down yet, knowing she'd be up in the night if she did. Everybody looked at me with a quiet sort of expectation. I wished Samuel were here to tell them all a good story. When we'd had them over before and things seemed so uncertain, his storytelling seemed to make everything a little easier. But I couldn't do it. Not the way he could. And anyway, a story would be best when everybody was ready to lie down. It wasn't even 6:30 yet. They weren't ready.

It might have been a good time to get everybody involved shelling and chopping nuts and mixing and shaping cookies. But that would take a while, and maybe wasn't the best project with a few upset stomachs in the house. But I had to do something to take their minds off of illness and the glaring absence of their fathers. And I caught a glimpse of a stray red Crayola that must have rolled into the corner when the rest of the box got put away. Franky's idea came to mind. I still wasn't sure if a stand-up paper nativity would be workable for us, but at least we could give it a try. Even if we accomplished nothing more than making a mess, it would keep the little ones busy.

I got out the scissors, paper, Crayolas, pencils. But what in the world could we use to hold the paper in its cone shapes? I thought I knew. I had the little girls' interest already, and they followed me to the kitchen cupboard to pull out a small bowl and a spoon or two of flour. Just a bit of flour-and-water paste ought to do the trick. And we could keep quite a few hands busy holding things in place until the paste was dry enough to set.

Oh, it would have been wonderful if we could have gotten the radio working to play some Christmas carols for us in the background. At least we would have had a lovely festive atmosphere. As it was, I had a difficult time convincing particularly the older children that this was a project worthy of their attention. Eventually Kirk and Willy abandoned us entirely and sat by the fireplace playing checkers. At least they were in the same room, and somehow, despite our numbers, I found that comforting tonight.

Lizbeth let Emmie play with a piece of paper and try her hand scribbling on it. She seemed to like that really well, and though she still seemed feverish, she wasn't fussy anymore. Franky cut out a circle with a slit on one side and showed the others how to make the cone bases. Joe and I became the designated "cone holders" while paste was drying. In no time we had seven little paper cones, some with lovely colorful scribbles.

"Them don't look like people," Harry observed.

"That's just the bottoms," Franky explained. "Ever'body wore robes then, so that's why it's okay to look so wide like that."

Sarah nodded. All this apparently made wonderful sense to her. "We have to put heads on."

"What heads?" Berty questioned immediately.

"We gots to make 'em," Franky answered. "I think I know a way." He cut a smaller rectangular piece of paper and rolled it to make a tube. I'd wondered how he'd thought to do that, but he'd worked it out in his mind, and I was impressed. A little paste held the paper tube together and a little more held it atop a cone in just the right place to be the head resting over a generously wide cone robe.

But Rorey wasn't satisfied. "He's got a hole in the top of his head. That looks really dumb."

"That's where you put a shepherd's hat or maybe some yarn for hair," Franky told her.

"They's still gonna have a hole in their head," the little girl complained. "Just covered up. An' a hole in the bottom too. Real big."

"Oh well," I said quickly. "I'm sure if we picked up our pretty little glass nativity and looked at the bottom, whatever the figures are standing on wouldn't look like feet. It's just for show."

"Can I see?" Rorey asked immediately.

"Well . . ." I hesitated, but surely if I kept our precious little figurine in my own hands it would be all right. I lifted it down from the mantel and turned it over carefully. "See. At the bottom of the robes there's nothing at all. It's even partly hollow."

"From the top it looks like Mary's kneeling," Sarah observed. "But underneath, she don't even have legs!"

"It's just for show, like I told you. A fun way to display the reason we celebrate Christmas."

"'Cause lidda Lor' Jesus is borned in a manger," Berty added.

"Right. Just like your song."

"Can I make the paper Jesus?" the little boy asked.

Franky frowned. "I been thinkin' 'bout that. He'll hafta

be smaller. I don't think a cone is gonna work right for him."

"Let's just work on some of the others for now," I suggested as I put the glass nativity away. "We can figure that out tomorrow."

"But we have to have a Jesus," Sarah began to protest.

"It's okay." Katie supplied the answer quietly. "He isn't born yet."

"Yeah!" Sarah's whole face lit up as though it were revelation. "It isn't Christmas yet!"

Rorey picked up a cone and turned it around in her hand. "These sure would smash easy."

Why did she have to be like that? I hoped to goodness she didn't take to destroying what was already made. Rorey had such an awful attitude so much of the time. But nobody else seemed to pay any attention.

"We'll have to make the manger bed for Jesus too," Sarah continued. "And some paper hay 'cause he's asleep on the hay. Only not yet, 'cause he isn't born yet. And some of these other guys have to be shepherds."

"And angels," Franky added, suddenly the expert. "We'll hafta make some more cones, so we can have plenty shepherds an' angels, plus the kings too. And those guys'll hafta have crowns on their heads."

Robert looked at me skeptically. "These might look awful funny."

"That's all right," I assured him. "I've seen unusual manger scenes in my life. I've even heard that in Russia they have one where all the pieces stack inside the biggest piece."

"Which one's biggest?" Harry wanted to know. "A really fat shepherd?"

"Or an angel big as the sky," Sarah supposed.

"Nothin's that big," Rorey contradicted again.

"I didn't mean really." Sarah shook her head. "It's just a saying."

Kirk and Willy finished one checker game and started another. I thought maybe Robert or Joe might want to play the winner of their first game and leave us to our paper creations, but neither of them said a word about it. Robert helped Berty paste a paper-tube head while Joe was helping Harry. Franky cut a few more rectangles to size. Sarah thought it might be easier to color on the faces before they were pasted, so she started adding eyes and merry smiles to a couple of Franky's rectangles. Katie claimed one too and said she wanted to make shiny angel faces. And Rorey seemed to be following their example. But soon Sarah was expressing dismay at Rorey's work.

"Why's that one frownin'?"

"'Cause he don't feel like smilin', that's why."

Sarah set her Crayola down and faced Rorey with a huff. "But everybody's happy about Jesus being born!"

"This here's a scared shepherd. 'Cause the angels showed up so sudden. He got startled out a' his bad dream, an' now he's wonderin' what's goin' on."

I looked Rorey's way and drew a quick breath. I hadn't expected anything like this, and somehow I felt that she was telling us something.

"That's not in the Christmas story!" Sarah continued her protest.

"It could be!" Rorey argued. "How do you know? Maybe

72

there was a shepherd sleepin'. How would you feel if you was sleepin' outside someplace, an' then a bunch a' folks in the sky started yellin' all of a sudden?"

"Excited, that's how I'd feel." Sarah pouted. "Mommy, tell Rorey the shepherds isn't supposed to frown."

"Honey," I tried to calm her. "It won't hurt to let Rorey make one the way she wants. It'd be perfectly under-standable for a shepherd under the circumstances to feel unsettled and a little afraid. Remember that the angel told them to fear not. It must have been pretty startling to see the angels there."

Rorey smiled, and I was glad to have even a little rea-son to back her up and not scold her for once. It seemed something of a miracle that she'd decided to participate in our little project, and I certainly didn't want her discouraged.

Sarah was not very pleased with me, however. "Well . . . okay. But all the shepherds shouldn't be frownin'. 'Cause some is thrilled. And none of the angels would frown. Not even one."

"I think that's right," agreed Lizbeth, who was holding a sheet of paper in place while Emmie scribbled over it in purple and green.

Rorey ignored them both and worked quietly for a while on her frowning shepherd. But then she took up another paper rectangle and drew another frowning face.

"Mommy!" Sarah protested as soon as she saw. "Look! Look what that Rorey did again! We told her only one frowny shepherd!"

"This here's a angel," Rorey said calmly and proceeded to draw teardrops dripping from one eye.

"Mommy!" Sarah looked like she could cry. "I want a happy manger scene!"

Lord have mercy! I was about to take both girls aside when Katie's quiet voice stopped me before I could speak.

"I unnerstand why an angel would be sad."

"Why?" I had to ask her, hoping that all this talk wasn't going to turn everyone's minds back to our grief and troubles.

Katie looked so small, and almost scared to have attention suddenly shifted onto her. "Didn't Jesus used to live with the angels in heaven?"

"Yes, honey. And he came to earth to save us."

"But maybe a angel is sad 'cause Jesus wouldn't be there now, so he wouldn't get to see him for a long time."

Franky suddenly nodded. "Maybe he even knew that Jesus was gonna die. Maybe the angel was sad about that too."

I might have expected such thoughts from him. Franky was often thinking and putting ideas together in surprisingly deep ways for his age. But little Katie? And Rorey?

"I must admit," I told them, "it does sound understandable. There may have been both tears and smiles in heaven on that day. But mostly smiles. I'm sure Sarah's right. It's okay, Rorey, to have one frightened shepherd, and one angel that's thinking about the sad parts of Jesus's life. But his birth was a joyous time, and a reason to celebrate— then as much as it is now. He left heaven and endured sad things to set us free. And now he's in heaven again, and there's no reason not to rejoice."

Rorey kept on drawing tears. "Does that mean you don't want no more'n two frowny faces?"

"I think two is all right among all the smiles," I told her gently. "But two is enough."

Beside me, Katie hung her head and covered her paper rectangle with one hand. "What's the matter?" I asked her. "Can I see?"

Slowly, without a word, Katie slid her hand away from her angel face. There in the corner of one eye, above a radiant orange smile, was a tiny blue tear.

She sniffed. "Do you want me to throw it away?"

"No. What a pretty happy face. Sometimes I cry a little when I'm happy."

"You do?"

I put my arm around her shoulders. "Sometimes joy gets so big you feel it's just running over inside you. And the tears come out, but it's still joy. That's another reason for an angel to cry, I guess."

Katie smiled. "My angel really is happy. About Jesus."

"That's good then," Sarah pronounced.

Rorey spent the rest of her time coloring an entire sheet of paper yellow to be cut in shreds for hay, so there was no more conflict over her interpretation of shepherd and angel faces. Katie and Sarah started pasting, and I held the little paper tubes in place until they would hold on their own. It was getting later now, and I was ready to start children on their way to bed, but Harry and Bert didn't think it would be right to leave so many cone people without their heads attached. So we glued all the parts together and started picking them up to set them in a safe place to dry.

"They all live in Bethlehem," Sarah said. "So we get to pick a place to be Bethlehem, right?"

"The kitchen table's the safest place with plenty of

room," I suggested. "So none of them get stepped on overnight."

"Then the table is Bethlehem!" Sarah declared with excitement.

"That's okay," Franky agreed. "But they don't really all live there. Joseph and Mary was just on the way for a while. An' the kings come to visit 'em from far off."

That was innocent enough information, and I doubt he could have imagined what he was starting.

"Oh!" Sarah started looking around. "Mommy, Joseph and Mary aren't ready to be in Bethlehem! Baby Jesus isn't here yet, and it's not Christmas Eve."

I shook my head, surprised that she seemed to be taking all this so seriously. "Honey, we're just setting these up out of the way so you all can go to bed."

"Can we put Mary and Joseph someplace else? Please?"

"Sarah—"

"And the kings," Berty joined her. "They's far off."

How could I argue? "All right. Whichever ones are Mary and Joseph, set them over on the cupboard."

"And the kings!" Berty repeated. "The kings!"

"How about the pantry shelf?" Robert suggested. He had a twinkle in his eye like his father's, and I knew he was enjoying the younger children's flight of fancy.

"Fine," I told them. "Take the kings to the pantry."

"Hey. That's even east," Franky announced to us. I was surprised he knew that, but I probably shouldn't have been. He'd surely heard someone talking about the directions out here, and he usually remembered what he heard.

Lizbeth and Harry moved Mary and Joseph to the cupboard. Robert took three more of the cone figures

76

away, and Sarah climbed on a chair and examined the rest. "Yep, these are shepherds and angels. Franky, is it okay for the shepherds and angels to be in Bethlehem already?"

He nodded. "The shepherds must live 'round there 'cause they gots their sheep grazin' close by. An' the angels is prob'ly gettin' things ready."

Sarah smiled. "Then let's move the shepherds over here." She scooted a couple of cone figures to the left. "Then the angels can stay here with Rorey's hay. They're trying to figure out how we can make the manger bed tomorrow."

"Are we gonna make sheep?" Harry asked.

"We need sheep," Berty immediately agreed.

"Oh, brother," Willy commented from behind me. "You guys get all carried away kinda stupid."

"No criticizing," I warned him. "I'm glad for us to get carried away in a little Christmas fun."

Lizbeth suddenly smiled just a tiny smile, the first I'd seen from her all day. But she didn't say a word.

"We can try to make sheep tomorrow," I told the little boys. "But that could be quite a challenge."

"I think one tube for the body, with legs glued on," Robert suggested. "And another tube for the head."

"Can we try it?" Harry wanted to know.

"Tomorrow," I repeated. "It's time for bed."

"But Daddy isn't home," Sarah protested.

Her words hung in silence for a moment. I saw the same angry uncertainty in Kirk's eyes and a painfully weary sadness in Lizbeth's.

"It'll be all right," I told them all. "He'll be home soon."

"Where is he?" Sarah persisted, and oh, I wished she hadn't.

"He's out looking for our pa," Willy said bluntly. "Who knows when he'll be back."

"Soon," Franky repeated my promise, but he suddenly looked scared.

"It'll be all right," I said again, not sure what else to tell them. "Come on, now. Everyone to bed."

Without a word, Lizbeth took Emmie and her little cup to the rocker.

"I wish we could have a story," Sarah said sadly.

I sighed, not wanting what had become a wonderfully uplifting evening to end on such a gloomy note. "Get the Bible storybook. I'll read to you about the birth of Jesus. It'll go right along with what we were doing."

Immediately, Berty started singing again. "Lidda Lor' Jesus as'eep on da hay! I know the story, Mommy!"

It jarred me terribly when he called me that. He was the only one of the Hammonds who ever did. He was so young. I hoped he wasn't already losing the memory of his mama. Somehow I couldn't bring myself to correct him and remind everyone again, though I knew the word had probably jarred his older siblings as much as it did me. "There's more to the story than the song, Berty. Everybody lie down or have a seat around the davenport and you'll see."

I read until little eyes were heavy and most of the story was done. "Let's finish later," I said softly. "Time for bed now."

"But we should finish the story now!" protested Harry, who seemed back to his old self again, not wanting to go to bed.

"It's good to leave a little for another time."

"Maybe for Christmas Eve," Sarah suggested. "Like baby Jesus. Can we read the rest the same night Jesus comes?"

I wasn't completely sure what she meant. "If you want me to read the Christmas story on Christmas Eve, that's all right with me. But off to bed now."

Sarah and Katie both gave me kisses and started for the stairs. Robert, Willy, and Kirk reluctantly followed them. Franky lingered only long enough to thank me for letting everybody work on the manger scene. And then I helped Joe settle Berty, Harry, and Rorey while Lizbeth rocked a squirmy Emmie to sleep on her lap. I made the rounds of every room, making sure all the children had adequate covers, and kissing my own and any of the others that I knew would appreciate it. Finally, when all of the lamps and candles were blown out but one and the house had grown quiet, I made my way to the kitchen and looked out a window, wondering where Samuel was right now and what, if anything, he'd found out about George.

Despite the children feeling better and the mostly happy evening we'd spent, I felt so torn, so tense inside that I could hardly hold back tears. Samuel should be home by now. What could be keeping him? Whatever it was couldn't be good.

Staring out across the cold darkness made me feel lonely, even with twelve children in the house. What would be next for the Hammonds? And even for us? *Lord God, we need you this Christmas.*

I let the curtain fall back to its place at the window and turned around slowly, wondering if Samuel would be home at all tonight, and what it meant if he wasn't. The single candle I'd left on the table shed enough light for me to see the shepherds and angels waiting on our "Bethlehem" table. Katie's little angel was the only one turned toward me, and I could see a hint of her features but not enough to discern the tiny tear I knew was there. *Oh, God, did your angels cry? Did you, on the night your son was born? What a gift! What a precious yet mind-wrenching gift you gave.*

I turned from the table toward the bedroom doorway, letting a few stubborn tears cascade slowly down. And out of the blackness, Berty's quiet, sleepy voice came floating.

"The lidda Lor' Jesus . . . as'eep on da hay . . ."

The Cattle Are Lowing

Some time in the night I heard the back door open and shut quietly. I slipped from between the covers, knowing it would be Samuel, and he would be hungry and cold by now. He was still by the door, pulling off his boots, when I entered the kitchen. I was on my way to the cupboard drawer to get a match when he took hold of my arm.

"Julia."

Just my name. Nothing else. I turned toward him, and he pulled me into his arms. He felt so awfully cold, like ice. I hugged him, felt his deep intake of breath, and he held me tight to his chest, still not saying anything more.

"What's wrong?" I couldn't wait. The silence felt like knives inside me. Was George still missing? Or dead?

"Juli, I'm sorry to be so long."

"Did you find him?"

"No. I tried. I wanted to come home hours ago, but I couldn't seem to let it go. Not after last year . . ."

I understood and reached my hand to his head. Samuel had found George back then, had stopped him when he'd been about to hang himself. All these Hammond children would have been fatherless then, if Samuel hadn't tried so hard for George's sake. And now I knew he was feeling broken, to have to come home alone.

"Surely he's all right. Just getting foolishly drunk someplace trying to forget—"

"I looked. Everywhere Ben and I could think he might have gone to find liquor or anything else."

"Ben Law?" The sheriff. Samuel was awfully worried to have called for his help. And rightfully so. "Surely George wouldn't do anything too stupid—"

"Suddenly leaving like this was stupid enough," Samuel replied. "Who knows what else he might do? He's been by Fraley's. And he got two quarts of Buck's home brew. That's enough to fell an ox. Who knows the shape he's in now?"

I squeezed him, petted his hair. "Honey, maybe he'll just sleep it off and then go home."

"We checked by there. Several times. Ben said he'd keep on checking, but there was nothing else I could do."

"There isn't. George is a grown man."

"Not really, Julia. I guess I've known that all along. I think Emma did too. That's why she wanted me to watch for him, and us to look out for his children. She knew he's no older than Franky inside somehow, maybe not even that old."

"Oh, Sammy."

"I'm serious. George is not all right, honey. I'm not sure he ever has been."

"But there's nothing else you can do. Not tonight. Please. Come and get some rest."

"What are we going to do?"

"He'll be home. It'll be all right."

He was quiet for a moment, and I felt his heart thundering in his chest as I held him. Samuel cared so deeply, so completely. I hoped there was some way George Hammond could understand what a gift it was to have such a friend. I'd thought he'd understood last year. He'd seemed to, to recover, to be grateful for life even, and the blessings God had given him and his children in enabling them to carry on.

But this was December, and George was thinking too much, remembering too much, about the bad things. Maybe Samuel was right. Maybe he was like a child somehow, unable to face all the responsibilities that went with being a father to so many. But despite such thinking, I recognized a touch of anger in me about it all. He was not a child. He was a man. With ten precious children who still needed him dearly. Despite the grief, despite the personal anguish, I could not help feeling that it was also a dreadful dose of selfishness that had him forgetting that his children were bound to be struggling too, and would struggle even more if they knew of his reckless, thoughtless behavior.

"Are you hungry?" I asked Samuel, trying to push the bitter thoughts from my mind.

"Yes. But I don't feel like eating."

"Let me make you a sandwich, honey. Please. Do you want me to warm up the soup and dumplings?"

"No. We should just go to bed. I don't want to wake the children. Is Harry feeling better?"

"Yes. They all seemed to improve. The doctor's medicine helped, I think, plus the rest. And getting their mind off things."

He suddenly kissed me.

"You kept them occupied, didn't you? Juli, you're so good with children. If . . . if he doesn't come back—"

"He will. Surely he will."

Samuel took a deep breath and pulled me with him toward a chair. "But if he doesn't . . ."

I felt like I was shaking inside. "What would you want?"

"These kids already look to us. Even the doctor and the school look to us, Julia, because they already know we're the ones making decisions. George just doesn't—"

"Maybe you're right. Maybe he can't."

He swallowed hard, struggled with the words. "But the kids lean on us. They're comfortable with us, mostly. And you know their relatives can't take them, at least not all of them together."

"And you would?" I asked, tears springing to my eyes.

"If you would. Can you imagine how they'd feel if we didn't? If they lost us too?"

"Oh, Sammy. This is just talk. They're not losing anyone. Surely—"

"But I needed to talk to you about this. Even if George does get home, we need to look at it. They've been staying with George, coming back and forth. We've seen so much of them, but I've still been trying to pretend like we're two separate families and we can just send them all home when

84

we want and be by ourselves. Now I just don't know. I think we need to keep in the middle of things. Keep seeing to them, even more, if they're going to stay together. And you know they need to. They want to."

"George's been all right up to now—"

"Not all right enough."

I let those words rest for a moment as I got up to light a candle and get him something to eat. I needed to soak in what he was telling me. I needed to decide whether my heart was willing to accept what he seemed to be asking of me. I'd already accepted the Hammond children. They were so much a part of our lives now that a day when we didn't see them seemed strange. But Samuel wanted to commit to more. At least in our hearts, in case the day should ever come when we were all they had left.

"Yes," I told him quietly. "If something were to happen to George, the children should be together." I turned back toward him. "They would need us to be steady, to be here for them just as much. And more than we are now. I would be willing to take them all in, if it ever has to be. And I'm willing too, to do what we need to do to make sure their needs are met, even when they have their father with them."

Samuel stood up and wrapped his arms around me. "Thank you."

"I'm just glad they still have their father. And I pray he's safe and in his right mind for Christmas and way before."

"Me too."

"Is just cheese all right on your sandwich?"

"Oh, Juli. I love you."

I never did get his sandwich made. Off somewhere in the house, we heard a clunk and the soft, muffled sound of a child's voice. Samuel started in that direction, and I lit a candle and followed him. Harry had fallen off the edge of the mattress onto the hardwood floor and was mumbling something incoherent in his sleep. Gently, Samuel lifted him onto the mattress again.

"Julia, he's burning up with fever."

I leaned close to touch his forehead. The poor child was sweaty hot, even though the room had gotten cool as the fire faded. He needed more of the medicine, but I hated to wake him. Samuel still had one hand on the boy's arm and his head bowed. Praying. What a blessing I had in Samuel. *God, thank you. Heal Harry. And any of the others if they are still sick.*

Emmie was snuggled close beside Lizbeth, her little arm sprawled almost over Lizbeth's face. She was warm too, but not so warm as Harry. Berty felt fine. Rorey was nearly as warm as Emmie. But they all slept soundly, comfortably, while Harry was tossing and turning. I was about to ask Samuel if he thought it would be wise to wake the boy to get medicine down him when I heard the soft sound of footsteps on the stairs.

It was the middle of the night. I was so startled, I spun around. Was another child sick?

"Mommy?" Sarah's quiet voice reached across the room.

"Yes, honey, I'm here."

"I got woked up 'cause Katie's crying."

Oh no. I turned to Samuel. "If you can stay close for Harry, I'll go."

In the candle's light, I saw his nod, and then I took Sarah's hand and climbed the stairs with her.

"Mommy, she don't talk to me when I asked her what was wrong. Is she sick too?"

"I don't know. Maybe she's not awake."

Apprehensive, I walked Sarah back to her room. Katie was curled on the bed next to the wall, holding her pillow against her chest and sobbing.

"Katie?"

I thought she may have quieted, just a little, but I wasn't sure.

"Honey, are you awake?"

A nod. Barely perceivable. I set the candle on the nightstand and eased onto the bed. Sarah climbed up beside me.

"Can you tell me what's wrong?"

She shook her head, tried to stop crying, but without much success. I reached to take her into my arms, and supportive little Sarah placed her hand tenderly on my shoulder.

"Mommy," Katie whispered.

"Were you dreaming about her again?"

The tears seemed to increase. "I wish you were my mommy."

What could I tell her? None of us had known what to do with a situation like Katie's. Her mother was still out there, somewhere. Alive and able to care for her child. Just unwilling. And yet she'd signed nothing, she'd told no one that she was truly willing to give her up. I petted the girl's hair. Katie had won my heart from the very first day. We had no way of knowing what her mother would do, or whether she'd ever show up again. But as far as I was concerned, Katie was ours. And everyone else seemed to want that too.

"It's okay, sweetie. You belong with us, and that isn't going to change."

Katie clung to me, her face and the front of her wavy locks already wet with tears. "But will Mommy come for Christmas?"

"Honey, I really don't know. I don't think so. We've heard nothing at all."

"Why doesn't she want to see me?"

She climbed up higher into my lap, pulling on my neck so hard it hurt. And then she seemed to be struggling for a full breath over the tears.

"I don't know," I told her. "I can't imagine. She's just thinking of herself right now, and what she wants to do."

"And her . . . boyfriends," Katie added. "She thinks about boyfriends."

"Maybe so."

"But she . . . she doesn't love me . . ."

I held her tight, rocked her a little. By the candle's light I could see Sarah's eyes now brimming with tears. "Katie, we love you," she said quietly. "I want you to be my always sister."

"We do love you," I agreed. "You're a very big part of our hearts now."

Katie struggled against the tears, wiping one cheek against the sleeve of my flannel nightgown. "Mommy used to sing to me . . . at Christmas. That was the only time she ever did sing just . . . just for me."

"What did she sing?"

"'S-silent Night.' She said her grandma used to sing it to her."

"I'm glad you have that good memory. I'm glad your mother has that good memory too."

"Can you sing it for me sometime?"

I almost choked with tears myself. How could a mother willingly walk off and leave her child? Would she think of her, now that it was December, whenever she heard that song? Would she wish she had her little girl with her to sing it to again? For Katie's sake, I wasn't really sure if I hoped so. Katie didn't seem sure either.

"Yes, I can sing it for you. Would you like to hear it now?"

She nodded.

"It's so late. If you're feeling better now, we should all try to get some sleep. Would you lie down again? You and Sarah both, and I'll sing to you. And don't worry. We will always be your family, Katie. No matter what happens, that will never change."

She seemed to relax, climbed back under the covers, and lay her head again on her pillow. Sarah stretched out beside her, and I covered and kissed them both. "You're my good girls," I told them. "Close your eyes."

Katie wiped her eyes with the corner of a blanket, and then Sarah took hold of her hand. They both closed their eyes obediently, almost at the same time. I closed mine for a moment too.

"Silent night, holy night . . ."

I sang softly so I wouldn't waken anyone else, and the hush in the house seemed almost dreamlike.

"All is calm, all is bright, 'round yon virgin mother and child . . ."

Katie reached her free hand forward to take hold of mine. I smiled.

"Holy infant so tender and mild. Sleep in heavenly peace . . . sleep in heavenly peace."

In a few moments, their breaths were as steady and peaceful as the song. I leaned, kissed their foreheads, and started to get up, sure they were both asleep.

"Thank you, Mommy," Sarah suddenly whispered.

"Thank you," I told her. "For being a good sister. I love you, sweetie."

"I love you too, Mommy. Good night."

"Good night."

I kissed her again and then went on downstairs. Samuel was still up So was Joe now, and Harry was sitting between them on the davenport.

"Harry was sick to his stomach," Samuel told me when I was near enough. "Fortunately there wasn't much in him to come out. Lizbeth went to get his medicine and a drink."

I looked around a little, trying to see any mess in the candlelight. "Do I need to clean up?"

"I got it already," Samuel said. "Is Katie all right?"

"She is now. I think a dream woke her."

"This is a sick night," Harry said sadly.

"You'll be okay, buddy," Joe told him.

Emmie rolled and fussed, and Joe moved to rub her back and try to calm her before she stirred completely. At the same time, Lizbeth came back in the room with a cup and a small bottle. "Oh, Mrs. Wortham, I wasn't sure if Harry should have the fever medicine tonight or the stomach remedy."

"The doctor said it would be all right to take both together if need be, and I think tonight that would be a good idea."

"Ahhh," Harry started to protest.

"You want to feel better, don't you?" Lizbeth questioned. "We all missed your crazy ruckus yesterday."

Harry nodded. "I guess I'm bad sick."

"Thank the good Lord you're not," Samuel told him. "Not really. This will pass."

"I hope it passes fast," he answered. "Like Kirky racing a horse."

I'd never heard any mention of Kirk racing before, but everyone knew he loved his father's horses. And anyone else's. "Absolutely," I agreed. "Hopefully you'll be back to yourself by morning."

"Will I hafta go to school?"

"No. No one's going tomorrow. That's what the doctor said."

Samuel looked up at me in surprise. "Well. A full house tomorrow."

"Yes."

"Sounds like a good time for me to get the radio fixed."

Now I was surprised. "If you could."

"We'll see."

I helped Lizbeth get Harry to finish his medicine and his drink and then coaxed him back to bed. By then, Emmie was fussy again, and Lizbeth picked her up and rocked her before her cries got loud enough to wake the house.

"Do you want me to settle her back down?" I offered.

"Oh no, Mrs. Wortham," Lizbeth answered. "You go back to bed. I'm used to this."

She was, no doubt. Little Emmie had been without her mother since she was seven months old, and Wila had been sick for quite awhile before that. But it saddened me for Lizbeth to have to seem so much like a parent. Had their father ever sat up with the baby at night?

"I'll take her," Joe told his sister. "You rest. I know you're not feelin' the best."

It had never occurred to me to feel Lizbeth's forehead while I was checking on the others. And she hadn't said a word. "Have you been feeling poorly too?" I asked her now.

"It's not so bad," she said. "Like Mr. Wortham says, it'll pass."

"Fever? Stomach?"

"Little a' both, I guess."

"Will you please take some of that medicine and lie down? Let me have the baby."

She hesitated, but she did as I asked, and I took Emmie in my arms. She didn't seem as warm as she had before I went upstairs, thankfully. But Lizbeth. Dear Lord. Everybody around here leaned on Lizbeth.

Samuel went quietly to the kitchen to put the medicine back in the cupboard. I sat in the rocker and sang softly with Emmie against my chest. Soon she drifted back to sleep. Harry too, though it took him a little longer. Then it was only Lizbeth and Joe still awake with us, the oldest two, except for the big brother we expected back home for Christmas.

It had taken Samuel a while in the kitchen, and when

he got back in the room he had a chunk of my homemade bread in his hand.

"Mr. Wortham?" Joe asked in a whisper. "What'd you find out about Pa?"

I could see Samuel's hesitation. But he answered. It wouldn't have been right not to. "Nothing, son. Not really. He's not home. I couldn't find out where he went."

"Drinkin'?"

"He got some liquor," Samuel admitted solemnly. "But he took off with it. I don't know where."

Joe got quiet. He hung his head, and I wished I could hug him. I stood to my feet carefully, hoping to lay Emmie on the mattress again so my arms would be free.

"Maybe he'll be back in the morning," Lizbeth told us, her voice sounding far away. "He'll have to sleep off the drunk, but he'll be all right."

"Not if he's still tired a' livin'," Joe said, an awful ache plain in his voice. "He tol' me that. He tol' me he was tired a' livin' without our mama. An' he didn't think he was doin' us no good anyhow."

"When was that?" Samuel asked.

"Month or two ago. I wondered then if it wouldn't get worse at Christmastime."

Samuel shook his head. "He promised me after last Christmas. He promised me he'd be here for you and do all he could."

"He did good for awhile, Mr. Wortham," Lizbeth said, her voice suddenly moving toward tears. "He really did."

I went to her. Samuel went to the davenport with Joe. There wasn't much we could tell them, or anything at all we could do, except to encourage them to be hopeful.

As far as we knew, their father was fine. He might well be home already, or at least home in the morning like Lizbeth said.

It was hard to get back to sleep that night, tired as we all were. Lizbeth and Joe were so brave, and shouldered so much for their younger siblings. I was proud of them both.

Morning broke over us windy and bright. Yesterday's snow blew and drifted and made piles and swirls outside where our garden had been. I was thankful it hadn't snowed enough to block us in, or get Samuel stuck somewhere else last night.

Berty, Emmie, and Rorey all seemed to have a touch of the fever when they woke, but not like Harry and Lizbeth. Both of them had wakened with chills and looking pretty miserable. I gave them more medicine and started a pot of chicken soup.

Berty was raring to go to work on our manger scene again, but I had to put him off till breakfast and cleanup were done and I'd seen to Lizbeth and Harry a bit. Samuel did chores by himself, and then left to take care of chores at the Hammond house, talk to Ben Law, and then check on the Posts and return their truck.

When I was ready, I moved paper, Crayolas, and all the figures we had in progress into the sitting room again, and most of the children started decorating the wide, cone-shaped robes or cutting out little pieces of paper to use for shepherds' headgear or kings' crowns. Berty hadn't forgotten yesterday's favorite song. But he seemed to get stuck on one line and sang it over and over. Finally he stopped and looked quizzically across the room at Lizbeth.

"What's lowing mean?" he asked her. "The cattle keep on doin' it in that song."

"I guess it's the same as mooing," she explained. "Don't know what else it could be." She sat up on the edge of one mattress with a blanket draped around her shoulders. I would have preferred her to try to lie down longer, but she wanted to be up. She wanted me to bring the manger scene work right here in the sitting room too, so we could spread out like yesterday.

"Why didn't whoever made up that song just say mooin' if the cows was mooin'?" Rorey questioned. "That woulda made a lot more sense."

"I think lowing is an old word for mooing," I tried to explain. "Like people used to say ye instead of you."

"The cattle are mooing," Berty started to sing, and then giggled. "I like that. Can we make cattle?"

"Goodness," I exclaimed. "Sheep are enough of a challenge to think about."

"But the song says there's cattle," the little fellow persisted.

"I suppose there were. And maybe we could try. But I just don't know. That seems awfully complex."

"The cattle are mooing," Berty sang again and then stopped. "We could makes 'em like sheep, only bigger! An' no woolly stuff on their sides."

"Do you have any cotton, Mrs. Wortham?" Lizbeth asked me.

"A little."

"I think I could figure out a sheep. And some cotton would make it look real nice. But cattle might be harder,

95

Berty. If we can make one at all, maybe it ought to be just one."

"One cattle," Harry laughed. "Our teacher'd say that weren't good English."

I appreciated the bit of humor from him. Hopefully it was a sign he was doing better. He was on the davenport again, wrapped in a blanket but watching us.

"I'm making Mary's dress especially beautiful," Sarah told me. "Because she's Jesus's mother."

"And I'm making this angel's dress beautiful too," Katie added.

"They's not dresses," Rorey corrected them both. "They's called robes. And angels don't wear pink." She tugged my sleeve and pointed at Katie's angel. "Look. That girl thinks angel robes is pink."

I only smiled. "I suppose angels can wear whatever color they want to wear, don't you? God surely likes all colors since he made such a colorful world."

"They's supposed to be white," she said with a sniff.

"Are you feeling all right?" I asked her, hoping not to have another day like yesterday with her.

"I'm fine, I guess. Not so icky in the tummy."

"Good. That's very nice to hear."

"Can we make cookies?"

I was very surprised Rorey would ask. She'd been less than enthusiastic when I'd mentioned the possibility yesterday. "Yes. But not right now. I'm hoping everybody will be feeling a little better first."

"An' we can finish all this," Franky suggested.

"Or at least a good bit of it."

"Where did Mary and Joseph come from again?" Sarah

asked me. "I know you read that part in the story last night, but I can't remember."

"Nazareth," Franky told her before I had the chance.

"Boy, Franky," she commented. "You're smart about this."

Rorey scoffed immediately. "He is not! He just remembered. So did I. He just said it first."

"Rorey," I warned her. "Do not start making ugly comments about anyone, or I'll sit you in the corner."

She sulked. She colored her shepherd's robe a streaky gray. But then she brightened a little and started putting stripes on her crying angel's robe. "These is going to need wings," she told me.

"We can do that. Eventually."

"Well, where's heaven?" Sarah suddenly asked.

"What?"

"If Nazareth is the cupboard, and the east is the pantry shelf, where's the heaven for the angels to come from?"

"Upstairs," Harry suggested. "That makes sense."

"Yeah!" Sarah's eyes were lit with enthusiasm again. "That makes sense."

By the time Samuel came home, we had three finished angels, complete with wings, and two nice-looking shepherds, one happy, one sad. Plus Mary and Joseph, each with little paper arms pasted on. And three tall kings with pointy-topped crowns. I wanted to put them all on the table again, together as a centerpiece where they'd be up out of harm's way. But Sarah whisked the angels away to run them upstairs to "heaven" so they could come swooping down from there again. Berty took Mary and Joseph back to the cupboard.

"I don't guess they's left yet," he told me.

And then Robert solemnly returned the kings to the pantry. "They haven't either," he said. "Of course not. Nobody made a star."

Samuel sat at the kitchen table with the milk and eggs from the Hammonds' farm, enjoying the children's merry antics and warming up with a cup of coffee. When the room cleared, he told me how glad he was that I could keep the kids so happy, rather than worrying about what was happening with their pa.

Ben Law had no word. There'd been no sign of George anywhere. But Louise Post was feeling a little better. And Barrett said we might need the truck more than he did. He'd sent Samuel home with it again.

"We need to do something extra special for them for Christmas if we can," I said.

"I'd like to," Samuel agreed. "But what do you have in mind?"

"Baking is the only thing I can think of. I'm sure they'd appreciate it. Louise may not be feeling up to it, and probably shouldn't be doing much."

"Do we have flour enough?"

"I hope so. But we're awfully low on sugar. I'm hoping to make holiday cookies with the children, but I'm just not sure how far it'll stretch."

He hung his head a little. I knew our lack had been awfully hard on Samuel all along. "Remember the little cedar box I made this fall?" he asked me. "I'll take it to town and see if the grocer won't trade."

I nodded. "We can spare a few eggs, and some of our

milk, I think. Since we have the Hammonds' here to use as well."

He looked at me uncertainly. And I didn't realize anyone else had heard. But Joe was suddenly standing in the doorway. "Take all the milk an' eggs to town you need. It's as much yours as ours anyhow. You've fed us more times than I can count. An' that ain't even half what you're doin'."

Samuel nodded to him. "It will help," he said. "To be able to buy a few groceries. Even just the sugar so your brothers and sisters can help make the cookies and things. They'll like that. Thank you."

Joe just sighed. "We're all in this together. I'm glad about that."

Again, I wanted to hug him, just as I'd felt in the night. But Berty came running in suddenly, and not far behind came Harry in his bare feet, swinging a pillow.

"Harry! Goodness, what are you doing? Where are your socks?"

"Didn't need 'em when I was layin' down."

I took the pillow from his hand. "Now that you're feeling well enough to be up, put your socks on. The floors are too cold to be running around without them. And no pillow fights. Especially in the kitchen."

"He put a angel on my head."

"Well, I can think of far worse things. Take care of those angels, please. The girls worked hard on them."

"Oh, Sarah's got 'em again. They's on the stairs practicing what they's supposed to say on Christmas Eve."

I could hear Sarah's voice just a little bit now as Harry

and Berty galloped away. And it sounded like Katie's voice was joining in the joyous song. I couldn't help but smile.

"Hark, the heral' angels sing! Glory to the newborn king! Peace on earth an' mercy mild! God an' sinners reconciled . . ."

They didn't seem to know any more of the carol. But I did. And I sang out the rest loud enough for them to hear me, much to their delight. They came running into kitchen, paper angels in hand. "Mommy! Mommy! You can be in the choirs of angels!"

Somehow, for just a moment, in the midst of these nativity-loving kids, I felt that I already was.

No Crying He Makes

Franky didn't run around the house and play like the other children. He was concentrating on the problem of how to make the baby Jesus and sheep that stood up. Finally he decided on a reverse design for the baby. A paper tube for the body and an inverted cone in the end of it for a head. He sealed the top with a circle of paper and wrapped his little "baby" with a blanket of paper, bringing one corner up "to keep his head warm." Sarah loved the little paper baby, but she was a little distressed, especially when I set the figure on the table.

"Mommy, it isn't Christmas. He isn't supposed to be borned yet."

"He was born a long time ago, sweetheart. We're just making a display—sort of like acting it out in his honor."

"But we want to act it out right, Mommy! He can't be in Bethlehem yet."

"Fine," I told her, just a little impatiently. I set the paper Jesus on the cupboard, next to Mary.

"That isn't right either," she complained. "Because he isn't borned." She whirled around and yelled, "Franky! Where was baby Jesus before he got borned?"

"In heaven, I guess," Franky answered simply, barely looking up from his second attempt at a sheep.

"Oh yeah. I forgot." She turned to me again. "Mommy, can I take him upstairs?"

I could almost have laughed, but I doubt she would have appreciated it. She was so straight-faced, like this was terribly important to her. "Sure. But when you're finished playing, please put it up so it doesn't get stepped on. Franky did such a nice job."

She ran off happily, and Berty suddenly came back in the kitchen and climbed into a chair. "I don't feel so good no more."

Not again. "What's the matter?" I asked him.

"I think I runned my stomach all jiggly."

I looked at Samuel with a sigh. "Just when I think we're getting on top of it."

He wasn't worried. "Nothing has kept Bert down for long."

"You'll have to sit awhile, or lie down," I told the boy. "Settle down and rest quietly. That was the point of no school for anyone today, after all. Not a giant recess."

"I don't get recess," he claimed. "'Cause I school at your house."

"You don't need recess," I informed him. "Because everything is play to you anyway."

Emmie was toddling about, holding Joe's hand. Harry was jumping on the stairs, evidently feeling much better. Rorey didn't seem so peppy, sunk in a sitting room chair with Sarah's doll on her lap.

"I want my own doll," she moaned.

I'd thought of that, and a change of clothes for all of them, but I'd forgotten to mention it to Samuel before he left. He thought of it now.

"Maybe I should take Joe with me into town," he said. "We wouldn't be long. And we can stop at their house and get a change of clothes and a few things."

"Can I come 'stead a' Joe?" Kirk asked immediately. "He's better with helpin' the little kids. I ain't no good at that."

Samuel was quiet for a moment, probably considering how Kirk would feel if they happened to find his father over there, or if they continued to find no sign. But Kirk already knew almost as much as Joe did. And he was almost as old. "All right," Samuel agreed. "Ask Lizbeth what all you'll need from over there."

Kirk made a face. "How long you think we'll be stayin' here?"

"I really don't know," Samuel answered.

"We could all go home without Pa."

But Samuel shook his head. "No. I'm sorry. You can't."

"Lizbeth is sick," Joe reminded him. "And she ain't no grown-up. Us neither. Jus' let it go. It wouldn't be right over t' home right now."

Kirk was solemn, but he said nothing more. Lizbeth was lying down again, her fever coming and going in waves. But

103

she gave him a list of what she thought he ought to bring. It was short. I thought that must mean she was hopeful, and I prayed George would come home today.

I made a grocery list for Samuel with the most important things on top in case they were unable to get everything. Surely the grocer would accept our milk and eggs, though we couldn't spare a large quantity of either. We'd taken some in to him once before. I could only hope he would also take Samuel's cedar box, but I had no idea how he would judge its value.

When they had left I diced onion for the soup pot and tried to come up with ways to engage the children in something just as engrossing as the paper manger scene. But I wasn't sure there was anything I could do to capture Willy's interest. At least he seemed to like Robert's company. Harry was feeling enough better to be restless. And Berty only sat in the chair a couple of minutes. At first I thought he must have gotten up because he was feeling better already, but I soon discovered that he'd gone in to snuggle on the mattress with Lizbeth. The little fellow was soon asleep at her side, fevering the way Emmie had been.

The day seemed to go that way, with Harry, Berty, and Emmie feeling better and then worse again alternately. Lizbeth got up and tried to act like she was fine, but I could tell she really wasn't feeling herself. Rorey stayed quietly out of sorts and to herself. I was glad when Samuel and Kirk got back with her very own doll. She seemed to perk up a little then.

They hadn't been able to get everything from the store, but what they did bring was a blessing. Especially the sugar. The grocer had wanted the cedar box and the eggs, but he couldn't use the milk because he already had so much. We'd not been the only farm family to bring some in to him. Samuel kissed me. He seemed relieved to be able to bring me groceries, but Kirk was very quiet. Ben Law had seen them in town and had stopped to talk for a moment. There was still no sign of George.

Where could he have gone in this cold, without a horse or vehicle? Why would he think that taking off this way would help anything at all? Surely he would still be carrying his miserable feelings right along with him, wherever he was. And he certainly wasn't making his children very happy.

I fed everybody that felt like eating, and then Samuel started working on the radio. It hadn't worked well for a couple of months, but he thought he knew what might help. Franky stopped working on sheep to watch him, but Sarah's obsession with the paper nativity hadn't faded. She worked on head coverings for Mary and Joseph, and an extra big star pasted to a long paper tube to stand up behind the manger scene on Christmas Eve.

"Where did you leave the baby Jesus?" I asked her, not wanting Franky's handiwork to get lost or crumpled underfoot in this full house of ours.

"In heaven," she answered me with a smile. "Up-stairs."

"Up off the floor, I hope."

"He's on my dresser."

But when she went to get him later because she wanted to add stripes to his blanket, she couldn't find the little figure. She looked on the dresser, under it, behind it, and all around. But she wasn't upset. "He isn't born yet," she told me again. "He'll be here in time for Christmas Eve."

Somebody had moved him, of course. But I didn't tell her anything more. It'd turn up, or we'd have to make another one.

That night, Samuel had the radio in order enough for us to listen to a couple of shows all the way through. That brought even the big boys' attention. I popped popcorn, and we all sat in the living room and enjoyed the Mystery Theater, and then Russell Bartlett and his Merry Christmas Band. Everybody seemed to be doing better by then, with no one else showing any sign of being sick. Praise the Lord for that.

The next day was Saturday. Only eight days to Christmas. Franky and Sarah decided that the pantry wasn't far enough east for the wise men, and the cupboard was too close to the table to be Nazareth. So the wise men were moved to the far east corner of the sitting room, and Mary and Joseph were moved to the chest of drawers just inside the door to our bedroom.

"When do they leave for Bethlehem?" Sarah asked.

"Prob'ly tomorrow," Franky said importantly. "Then we can move 'em a little closer every day."

They worked together at producing some sheep for the shepherds, finally using skinny paper tubes for the legs. It took awhile to get the paste to hold, but finally the funny-looking little sheep could stand up on their own. Lizbeth helped them use a little cotton for the sides, and I was glad that I'd saved back a piece in a drawer. I helped them use the same design, only a little bigger, to make cattle. Two, because Harry insisted we couldn't have only one.

That afternoon, baby Jesus turned up in Robert's room, though none of the big boys admitted to moving it. Sarah was delighted that the baby'd been found. But she still maintained that he couldn't possibly stay with the other figures yet where he'd be easier to keep track of. She took the little thing back to her room, holding it in her hands as though they were a rocking cradle, and taking up Berty's song.

"The little Lord Jesus, no crying he makes . . ."

"He don't cry 'cause he's happy 'bout Christmas," Berty decided.

And I agreed. But despite the cheer in the younger children, I could sense an increasing heaviness among the older ones. I felt it in myself too. The closer we got to Christmas, the more they would all think of their mother. And, of course, their father too. *Blast it all, George Hammond! Where are you?*

Katie was extra clingy to me, and spooked easily when she heard a noise outside. I wasn't sure how to make her feel more at ease. Tucking the children in that night was difficult. We'd been carrying on so well, and yet a solemnity seemed to be settling over us. Emmie cried herself to sleep. Berty pouted a bit and asked about his pa. Willy had gotten downright cranky. By the time I got everyone to sleep, I was completely exhausted, and yet I knew I couldn't rest my head yet.

Samuel and I both stayed up late, working on gifts for the children. I was making Sarah and Rorey doll dresses, and a doll of her own for Katie so she could play along with them. Samuel was bending some stiff wire tonight, making fishhooks for Robert and Willy, who took the opportunity to fish whenever they could, regardless of the weather. We knew they'd like them. They'd had only one hook apiece before. One broken at the tip, and one rusty.

I'd already finished the blouse for Lizbeth by now, re-working one that had belonged to an elderly woman from our church. I had decided to make handkerchiefs for Kirk and Joe, and a tie for their older brother. Samuel had begun a little wooden truck for Berty with thread-spool wheels. And a bunch of clothespin soldiers for Harry. But I hadn't even started a gift for Emmie, and neither of us knew what to do for Franky. We had so little time left.

I felt like I could drop by the time we finally stopped to get ready for bed. But I took the time to walk through the house, checking on the children and praying. Somehow I felt almost lost, like all my efforts could not possibly be enough, and the holiday would end up dreadfully sad despite everything. *Oh, Lord God, be with us. Be with me.*

Wearily, I went on to bed, glad for the opportunity to rest my head on the soft pillow, even though the bed itself wasn't such a comfort with the mattress pulled off and lying in the next room. But tonight I knew I was too tired to care much about that. I figured I'd be asleep almost instantly. But my foot sliding beneath the sheets seemed to find something that didn't belong. Reaching down with one hand I found what felt like a roll of paper. Thankfully, Samuel hadn't blown out the candle yet, or I might have crumpled it without thinking. In the dim light, I could see what it was. Franky's little paper baby Jesus. How he'd gotten in our bed, I might never know.

I Love Thee, Lord Jesus

The next day was Sunday, and I'd thought we'd go to church, but it was snowing again, Rorey still wasn't feeling well, and now Joe seemed to be coming down with a touch of the flu too. Lizbeth said she was fine, but I wondered. Emmie was doing better than she had been, but she still felt a little warm. Samuel and I decided it was best to keep everybody home.

I was sitting at the table, listing the things I'd like to bake for us and for the Posts when Lizbeth suggested that we make something for our pastor and his wife too.

"They was so good to us last year, and they don't have much."

She was right. We had shared cookies with them before, so I had an extra incentive to make plenty again. But that didn't have to be all. A loose button on my sleeve sparked an idea that turned out to be a way to keep a few restless children occupied again.

I got out the button jar. I didn't even have to say anything; just the sound of me dumping them on the table brought curious children to see what I was up to. So I sat and showed them how to thread through more than one of a button's holes so the fronts would stand out. Enough of them strung in a line would make a bright and distinctive necklace for the pastor's wife. Katie loved it.

So did Sarah. "Can we make one for our teacher too?"

I happily agreed. But since Katie, Rorey, Sarah, and Bert were all working on separate strands, we were definitely going to have extra. Lizbeth sat and helped them when their little fingers had trouble with small holes, and she sorted the buttons by size and color too, encouraging the younger children to use nice combinations instead of just haphazardly threading at random. They'd have some nice necklaces when they were finished.

I asked Robert if he and Willy could make a gift for the pastor. I'd seen a nice Bible bookmark once, made of several strips of colored ribbon to mark more than one page at a time. I thought perhaps we could come up with our own design. Willy wasn't at all happy with the idea. Me sitting them down with pieces of ribbon seemed to insult him, but Robert liked the challenge. Eventually, Willy and Kirk went outside to bring in firewood, and Robert worked on an idea with Franky instead of Willy at his side.

I had five different colors of ribbon, so they cut a piece the same length from each color and decided to use an empty thread spool to hold them all together at one end.

The ribbons all went through the hole and were knotted together on both sides of the spool so it would stay in place. That was simple and easy but not good enough for those boys. Franky suggested notching the edges of the little wooden spool and carving a cross into the side of it. Robert pulled out his pocketknife and started right away.

"Can I make one for Mr. Wortham?" Franky whispered to me. I was happy to agree and got him another little spool.

I'd thought Harry had been with Joe in the sitting room while most of this was going on, but when I checked on him and his napping baby sister, I found the little boy on the stairway tumbling a paper wise man down the steps.

"Harry, be careful with those."

"They's goin' down the mountain."

Surely he was the one who had been moving the paper Jesus. I asked him, but he didn't own to it. He sent another wise man rolling down and then suddenly looked at me with his dark eyes full of question.

"Do we live here now?"

"You're staying with us," I answered vaguely. "I hope that's all right with you."

"What's Pa doin'?"

How I wished I knew! It wasn't easy to answer. "Right this minute, I'm not sure. Maybe he's thinking to have some lunch like we should."

"Is he comin' over for lunch?"

"He's welcome," I answered, rescuing the two wise men I could reach and turning away. "Will you bring the other wise man down from the mountain?" I asked him. "Then you can help me wash potatoes."

111

"Oh boy! Can I use the big washtub again?"

I'd let him and Bert do that once before, and I knew very well I was in for a mess, but I didn't care. Somehow it seemed worth it to let them have fun helping me. So I spread out towels next to the kitchen stove and set the washtub on top of them. I dipped in only about an inch of water and gave Harry all the potatoes I thought we'd use. Berty climbed down from his place stringing buttons to help in this delightful project. The potatoes soon became sailing ships, sharks, and whales, and they were all sloshed through the water enough to get any remaining garden dirt off them easily.

Samuel led us in Bible reading after lunch, because it just seemed right since we hadn't been to church. It seemed natural to sing too, like we did at church, so I led a hymn.

"Can we sing a Christmas carol too?" Sarah asked.

I chose "Silent Night," mostly for Katie's benefit, but Berty wasn't about to let the opportunity go by to sing his favorite, so I let him lead us in "Away in a Manger" too. We'd just begun the second verse when Sarah suddenly jumped up and ran for the stairs.

"I forgot! Jesus is with us at church!"

I wasn't sure how I felt about her taking that little paper figure so seriously, but when she came down the stairs cradling it carefully in her hand and still singing, my eyes filled with tears.

"I love thee, Lord Jesus," she sang, and then looked at me with her bright eyes shining. "I know the real Jesus is grown up in heaven, Mommy. But I like to pretend."

I nodded.

112

Samuel smiled. "Not only in heaven," he said softly. "But with us every day."

"In our hearts," Sarah added.

We prayed. Franky asked us to pray for their pa, and we did, though I knew that calling his absence to mind so strongly was painful.

"Do you think he'll be here for Christmas?" Rorey asked solemnly.

"No," Kirk answered immediately.

"There's no way we can know right now," Joe softened the words. "We can jus' keep prayin' for him."

"I don't think he cares about that," Willy added cynically.

"Maybe not," Joe acknowledged. "But God does."

Franky nodded. Lizbeth too. And Berty took up singing all over again, rolling down from his chair to the floor with strains of "Away in a Manger" following him.

"I love thee, Lord Jesus . . ."

The words stuck in my mind. I remembered a Bible verse that said all things work together for good for those that love the Lord.

That's us, I prayed in my mind. *I don't know about George, just like Joe said. But it certainly applies to his children. Work good for them, Lord God. And for Katie. It's not her fault that her mother ran off chasing selfish dreams. Bless them, Father in heaven, each and every one of them. Bless all the dear children in thy tender care . . . They are in your care, Lord. I know it. Lighten our hearts. Make a way.*

Samuel had been going back and forth to take care of chores at the Hammond farm every day now. The older boys were certainly capable, but he didn't let them go alone, because he couldn't be sure what they might find. I thought he was afraid George might come back drunk and out of his head. But he confessed to me when we were alone that he was troubled by dreams of George trying to hang himself again, with this time one of the boys to find him, and they were too late.

I tried to assure him that George wouldn't do something like that. But how could we know for sure? This was the third full day since he'd left. Samuel had made a telephone call in town when he went for groceries, to let the uncle and the oldest Hammond boy know what was happening here, but he'd had to leave a message with a neighbor there, and we'd heard nothing more.

But just at twilight that Sunday evening, we heard a vehicle outside. The sound was enough to stir everyone. Some of the children were excited, thinking it might be their father. But others seemed as apprehensive as I felt. Ben Law might be bringing some word. Who could know? But it was the oldest Hammond boy coming in, without bothering to knock, just like his siblings. All of the Hammonds ran to greet him. We'd always called him young Sam, just to distinguish him from my husband. But he was hardly a child anymore at seventeen. Nothing animated the little Hammonds like Sam's arrival. What a godsend! It lifted even my spirits to have him home.

He was all smiles and hugs for his brothers and sisters. It'd been a month since he'd gone to help his mother's brother-in-law, but despite the kinship, that uncle just dropped him off and drove away without coming inside to see the rest of the children. I gathered that was his way of letting us know he'd answer the need here only by bringing Sam back, nothing more.

Sam didn't ask any questions at all. He only slid his bag into the corner, hung up his coat, and then went into the sitting room to romp and tussle with Harry and Bert. It was good to have him back. Only when the younger children were in bed did he sit down with Samuel and Lizbeth and me to talk things over.

"When did Pa leave?"

"Thursday," Samuel told him. "We know he got liquor, but not what happened or where he went after that."

The big boy sighed and shook his head, glancing over at Lizbeth. "I hate to say it, but I ain't sure we can count on him comin' back."

"We been prayin'," Lizbeth maintained. "And we can sure hope."

He didn't acknowledge her words. "I've got a little money. Not much, but at least it's somethin'. I almost stopped an' got the Christmas candy, Lizbeth, but Uncle Billy didn't wanna take the time."

"You shouldn't!" she protested. "Pa does that. Every year. That's what he gets us, since we were little."

Young Sam only sighed. "There's just no tellin' about this year."

"It wouldn't seem right, not comin' from Pa."

"Better than the little ones not havin' it at all."

Young Sam talked to us about what might come next for their family, and Samuel told him about our decision to help them, even if it meant taking them all in permanently.

"I ain't far off from eighteen," he told us. "We can make it if we hafta."

I knew all of us felt drained by the time we went to bed. I rolled out a pair of quilts to make an extra bed for Sam on the sitting room floor. Lizbeth was teary, but I knew it was sadness more than sickness troubling her now. And like some mysterious little touch of grace, she was the one who found the baby Jesus under her covers that night.

Look Down from the Sky

The children who were well enough had school on Monday and Tuesday, and then they were out for the rest of the week. By then everyone was feeling better. Sunday's snow was enough to cover everything generously, so on Wednesday afternoon, young Sam took his brothers sledding on the sleds Samuel had made last Christmas. I had thought that the little girls would want to go too, but they didn't, so I had them help me make bread for the Posts and then start some cookies—a triple batch of snickerdoodles to begin with.

Despite the rich smells in the house when the sledders came back, there seemed to be a somber mood among them. I discovered later that they'd been far enough into the timber to come close to the site of their mother's grave.

117

They hadn't gone there, but the snow, the cold, the barren trees—just like the day we'd buried her. It had been close enough to call it all back to mind. Wila Hammond and Emma Graham, gone together—it was a year ago last night. I knew at least some of the children realized that, and I wished I knew some comforting words to tell them.

I gave everybody the first cookies out of the oven and made cocoa to go with them. But the mood didn't improve much despite how quickly the treats disappeared. Samuel and young Sam had already left to do the milking and other chores at the Hammond farm for that evening, and I was left with the rest of them all just sitting around.

"Let's make the special Christmas cookies next," I suggested. "The roll-out ones with all the nice shapes you like."

"Trees," said Berty.

"And candy canes," Rorey added without much enthusiasm.

"And stars and angels," Lizbeth continued more cheerily. "I think that's a great idea."

She worked valiantly at getting everyone involved. Mixing or rolling, stirring the red coloring into a bowl of sugar, or grinding nuts and chopping dates and candied cherries to decorate the tops.

We made quite a production team, though I knew there were really very few hearts in it today. Lizbeth carefully cut out triangles, laying one sideways atop another to make a star. Then she showed the little girls how to make angels with a triangle, a small circle, and a large circle cut in half for wings. They used tiny bits of cherry for the mouths and date pieces for eyes. Katie added hair of finely ground walnut bits.

I looked to see if Rorey's angels were smiling today, but it wasn't easy to tell. "Do they have cookies in heaven?" she suddenly asked me.

"I don't know, honey," I told her, almost afraid to answer.

"This one's for Mama," she said soberly. "Do you think we could put it out with a note on Christmas Eve? Maybe Santa could take it to her. Don't he know the angels?"

I nearly choked up, and Lizbeth did, poor girl. But before either of us could speak, Kirk answered far too harshly, "Santa don't know no angels! He ain't even real! You can't give no cookie to Mama."

"I can too!" Rorey answered back, her eyes suddenly brimming. "On Christmas I can! Cause Mama said once anythin' can happen on Christmas! It don't matter what you say! It don't even matter if Santa is real!"

I don't know where in the world Kirk got such a mean streak, but the next thing he said seemed designed to tear at her. "I'm gonna eat that cookie. Soon as it's baked."

"No, you are not!" Rorey screamed. "It's Mama's!" In a fit of tears she flew off the chair where she'd been standing and rushed at him. I knew Rorey was one fiery little girl, but I'd had no idea she'd have no hesitation taking on a brother Kirk's size. She beat at him good, and he shoved her. Lizbeth, Joe, and I all hurried to grab them both before things could get any further out of hand. Joe was the one that got hold of Kirk first, and what surprised me more than anything else was that Kirk took an actual swing at him. I wished to goodness Samuel were here.

"What's the matter with you?" Joe demanded. "It don't hurt nothin' for a little kid to dream! Let her be!"

"It's just dumb. It's nothin', an' you know it! Do you think it's gonna help anything?" Kirk yelled at him. "Do you? Mama's dead! And Pa's been 'bout the same as ever since! There ain't no use pretendin' otherwise!"

As if she understood far better than we realized, Emmie burst into tears. She wasn't the only one. Katie and Sarah were soon crying too, along with Berty. Harry mashed the cookie he'd been working on into a squishy lump, and Willy set down the nut grinder and took off outside.

Robert followed Willy, grabbing both of their coats. I was so grateful he did. I had my hands full here. Rorey was still kicking and swinging, trying to get at Kirk. "You're not gonna eat that cookie! You're not!"

"Oh, hush," he told her. "You're just dumb."

"No, she's not," Franky said. He looked so pale and drained all of a sudden. His silvery eyes were dark and pained. "She was just bein' nice."

"You're dumber'n she is."

"That's enough!" Joe insisted, pulling Kirk toward the sitting room door. "What the devil's the matter with you?"

"I'm sick of it!" Kirk answered. "I'm sick a' pretendin' everythin's all right. It ain't! Why can't somebody just come out and say so?"

Joe dragged his brother into the other room, and I let them go, knowing there was nothing I could say right then that Kirk would want to hear. Lizbeth looked absolutely beaten. She drew in a deep breath and rested her hand on a chair back as if to steady herself.

"It is too Mama's cookie!" Rorey kept right on arguing

even though there was no longer anyone to argue with. She tried to pull away from me, but I was afraid to let her go. Lizbeth stirred herself to try and comfort Emmie and Bert. Franky, dutiful as a little soldier, put his arm around Harry as the smaller boy took another wad of dough and squished it soundlessly in his hand. Still Rorey struggled to pull away. I knelt and drew her into my arms.

"Rorey, sweetie," I said gently. "It's your mama's cookie and nobody's going to argue. Kirk's just upset, that's all. Sad and scared—"

"Scared?" she asked. Her eyes were angry, but her face was wet with tears.

"Yes. Big kids and grown-ups get scared sometimes when bad things happen. It's pretty normal, and it's okay. We just need to be patient with Kirk and try to understand. He misses your mama too. He just doesn't know how to deal with everything right now."

"Does he miss Pa?"

Her question made me cold inside. "Yes. I'm pretty sure he does."

She struggled with the next words and almost couldn't say them. "Is . . . is Pa dead too?"

Harry acted like he didn't even hear us. Franky stayed beside him, but he was watching me, his eyes seeming all the more haunted. Sarah and Katie were watching me too, motionless, like they weren't sure what to do. Berty spilled the bowl of red sugar, and Lizbeth took both of the younger ones into the bedroom and shut the door.

"I don't think he is," I answered Rorey plainly. "I hope not."

"Why did he go away?"

"I'm not sure anyone can explain. Not well enough. Just that he's so sad inside that he doesn't know what to do."

"He should come an' eat supper with us," she said with an easy logic I couldn't deny. "He should help me make another cookie for Mama. And one for Emma Graham too. Will you help me?"

It was a rare moment for Rorey, and I knew it was an important one. "Of course I'll help. You tell me what you want me to do."

"We need angels," she said solemnly. "Lots more angels."

Sarah and Katie helped me cut out more triangles and big and little circles. Franky stayed at Harry's side, letting him shape and then demolish the same couple of cookies over and over. We filled a cookie sheet with bare angel shapes and then started on another tray. I wasn't sure anybody would be able to eat these cookies, but right then I didn't care. Rorey needed angels. Maybe the rest of us did too. So angels we made. And once I figured out what it was that Kirk needed, I'd surely work on that too.

The bedroom door opened, and Berty came padding softly out in his sock feet. He helped me clean up the red sugar, and then he wanted to help decorate the tray of angels and I let him have his way. So did Rorey. She didn't care if they had sugar on them or how much or what color. She didn't care if they had eyes or mouths, so long as they were angels and no one touched the special one she'd designed for her mama.

Soon we were putting them in the oven and then pulling them out again to cool. Beside the stacks of snickerdoodles rose piles of Christmas angels.

Rorey surveyed our work and was satisfied. "I think Mama's gonna look down from the sky and be happy. She still loves us."

"Yes," I agreed. "Of course she does."

"Jesus look down from da sky too," Berty added solemnly, and I gave him a nod and a little squeeze.

We must have made Samuel and young Sam wonder when they came back bringing the Hammonds' milk again. Of course they wanted to get their hands in the cookies. Who wouldn't after working hard out in the cold? But I directed them to the snickerdoodles. For now, I thought we'd better leave the angels alone. Until Rorey was ready. Maybe until she'd put up her mama's and wanted to taste one herself.

The moment came a little sooner than I expected. Joe and Kirk came back in the room, Kirk with his head down and Joe prompting him on. Rorey stopped and stared at them, not about to back down.

"Sorry, kid," Kirk told her. "If you wanna do stuff in honor of Mama—even make a cookie—it's okay with me."

She stared for a moment. And then she reached for the cooling rack and grabbed an angel with a walnut nose and a generous supply of sugar covering the wings. She handed it to Kirk.

"Mama wants you to have one too."

After that, it was all right to eat them, with only a special handful set aside.

Samuel said Robert and Willy had been chopping wood in the yard. They came in quietly after awhile and didn't say a word about the outburst. Joe and Kirk went out together to see that the rest of the chores were finished.

Berty said Lizbeth and Emmie had both been crying when they went into the bedroom. When I went and checked on them, they were both asleep. But even in rest, Lizbeth looked weary and distressed. It was hard for me not to be angry about how wrenching all of this must be for her. Not at God, but at George, even though he hadn't asked for the loss of his wife any more than the rest of us had.

I felt so drained of energy that evening, I was glad I'd had another pot of soup simmering on the stove that didn't need further attention. After dinner, we all gathered to listen to a radio show again. Emmie and Lizbeth were even up to join us, and I was glad for the togetherness and the peace. But everyone was so quiet, like we were all afraid to say much of anything. Appropriately, the show we listened to signed off with a new rendition of "Away in a Manger." And strangely enough, that night it was Rorey who found the paper baby Jesus on the pillow beside her dolly.

Stay by My Cradle

All week, Mary and Joseph kept progressing a little closer to the kitchen table "Bethlehem." Most of the time, a group of the younger children would move them together, just a foot or two, with great ceremony.

"They're getting closer," Sarah would announce, and indeed they were. I thought their position on the hallway floor a little too precarious at times and would set them up out of harm's way when I knew there'd be plenty of traffic shuffling through. But whenever I did that, they always returned to the same spot before much time had passed. I assumed it was Sarah who put them back, but I never saw for sure.

Likewise, when I moved angels, shepherds, and livestock off the table to make room for a meal, no one said anything.

But I never had to put them back after cleanup. They just appeared, every time, when I was busy doing something else. Once I caught Harry and Bert moving them, but I know they weren't responsible every time. And nobody admitted to moving baby Jesus at night. He didn't show up in somebody's bed all the time. Sometimes he was on Sarah's dresser, the spot she'd designated for him. Sometimes he was just missing, only to show up the next day in the strangest of places. Samuel's boot. Joe's coat pocket. Even atop the tray of cookie angels.

Our wise men hadn't moved because nobody was sure when they saw the star and began their journey. Finally Robert decided that they'd better get started. So he helped the littler kids erect a simple paper stable with rolled paper legs, so they could paste the tube holding the star to the back of it. I was proud of all the work they'd done, but they still weren't satisfied. Franky, Sarah, and Katie fashioned the manger itself, while Rorey sat beside them, carefully tearing to shreds the sheet of the paper she'd colored yellow days ago. The stage was set.

The last few days before Christmas whisked by us without any more word about what had happened to George. It was hard not to give up, but Lizbeth still prayed every night that he'd come home to them. I knew Samuel was right that even if he did, we would need to stay close, keep a watch on things, and be here for the children.

Lizbeth and young Sam argued after the little ones were asleep, about whether Sam should go to town and buy the Christmas candy. Lizbeth seemed to feel it was too soon to accept that their father wouldn't take care of that for himself, and even if he didn't, it just wouldn't be right for the familiar striped candy sticks to come from someone else. So Sam finally decided that he would get a completely different kind of candy, something new to all of them, just "so the little kids'll have sweets" without duplicating his father's tradition.

He rode a horse into town alone for that, and on the same day we took the Posts three different kinds of bread, a pie, and a plate of cookies. They surprised us the following afternoon with a huge turkey, two crookneck squash, and four jars of home-canned corn. Here was our Christmas dinner! I tried to tell Barrett we'd only meant to bring them a gift to thank them for the use of their truck and for being such good neighbors. They didn't have to reciprocate. But he said they were just giving a gift too, to thank us for Samuel's help with the furnace and for being such good neighbors back to them. I sent Louise one of the button necklaces the children had made, plus a bag of mint leaves harvested last summer from the abundant supply behind the house.

Sarah and Katie had made Christmas cards for their grandmothers. I truly didn't expect to hear back from either one of them, but we did. Samuel was amazed that his mother sent a card. She'd only written to us once before, ever. And Katie was excited and scared all at the same time to receive a card from her mother's mother. She waited anxiously as I opened it to read to her, but there was no word in it about where her mother was now.

The day before Christmas Eve, Samuel took the children out to get a tree. Wisely, he went to the timber below the west pasture, avoiding the east timber between us and the Hammonds' house with the little grave site it contained.

The absences were hard enough to bear without visiting graves in this season.

I popped popcorn again, and the kids sat and threaded masses of it into a garland to circle around the tree. We put up Emma Graham's lovely glass ornaments and the yarn people and button ornaments we'd made last year. The big paper star from last year's tree had gotten pretty crumpled, so Rorey made a new one. Still, the tree looked a little bare, and last year's paper chain was now gracing the mantel, so Lizbeth got the kids making more paper chain, colored bright. And I wrapped a big red towel around the tree base.

That night very late, Samuel was working in the barn, finishing Berty's gift as I stitched on a cloth teddy bear for Emmie, cut from a worn-out old sweater. I'd already helped Samuel put the finishing touches on Harry's clothespin soldiers, and they were stretched out on the table in front of me with their painted faces and wooden-spool stands drying.

But we still hadn't figured out what to make for Franky, and we were running out of time. I thought I could just give him the hankies I'd made at his suggestion for his father, but I knew that would serve as nothing but a sad reminder. I was stewing a little about what else we could do when Samuel came in with his eyes twinkling merrily and one hand behind his back.

"Guess what I found."

"What?"

"It was in the corner of the hayloft, underneath that stack of old boards I'd been meaning to move." He pulled his hand forward. A hammer. A rusty, old, child-sized hammer. "It must have belonged to Emma Graham's son."

I took it in my hands, looking at him with question.

"I can clean it up. It's perfect for Franky."

"What on earth made you look in the hayloft?"

"Remember what he told us? About giving him some wood? I thought maybe we'd have to do that. I'd gone up to bring down some of those boards and pull the nails out, thinking to give him enough lumber and nails to make a little chair or box or something."

"Oh, Samuel, do that. Along with the hammer. He'll love it."

I made fudge late that night so I could surprise the children with it Christmas morning—an extra big batch so I could give extra to Sam and the other big boys.

I was finally ready to go to bed when Berty's quiet tears from a sitting room mattress caught my attention. He'd been so holiday-cheerful most of the time, but I really wasn't surprised to think that now in the darkness so close to Christmas he was suddenly feeling overcome. I went to his side, and he climbed from the covers and into my lap.

"What's wrong?" I whispered.

"I miss my folkses," he told me. "Bof' of dem."

I hugged him, knowing all too well how he felt. I could remember a long-ago Christmas when I was just a little tike, after my mother had died and my father had gone away. It was too familiar, and I wondered why the parallel had never dawned on me before. I squeezed him tight, feeling strangely stricken.

"Is you crying, Mrs. Wortham?"

"A little bit."

"Me too."

Oh, I loved this child. His simple, direct way of dealing with everything. I loved all of them. Even Kirk and Rorey in their difficult times. How could their father stand to be away from them? Tomorrow would be Christmas Eve! *May the realization of that work on his insides and draw him back. If he is still alive. I pray that he is!*

I tried to coax Berty to lie down again, but he didn't want to let me go.

"Stay wif me, please, Mom. I need you."

So I just kept holding him, tired as I was.

"Sing?" he asked me.

"Right now? Honey, I don't want to wake anyone else."

"You can sing real quiet. It's okay."

I petted his tousled brown hair. This little four-year-old claimed me with his whole heart. He even called me Mom. And who could blame him, really? I wasn't sure I should encourage it. I wasn't sure how to react with all of these Hammonds sometimes. But right now when it was surely already the wee hours of Christmas Eve morn, I couldn't refuse him. "What do you want me to sing?"

I should have already known. The only song he'd had on his heart for more than a week now. "'Away in a Manger.'"

I smiled. "All right. Do you want to sing along? Softly?"

"No." He shook his head. "Dis time I listen."

So I sang for him, as quietly as I could, through the first verse and into the second.

"Is that song wrote by a baby?" he asked me suddenly.

"No." I laughed a little, wondering at his question. "Why?"

"Cause it says 'stay by my cradle.'"

"I guess that can mean anybody's bed."

"Like this mattress right here?"

"Sure."

"Then you is stayed by my cradle."

"I guess I am."

"I'm gettin' tired again."

"I should think so. I am too."

"Can you stay by my cradle anyhow?"

Even in the darkness I knew the tears in his eyes. He clung to my hand as he eased himself back down into the covers next to Harry. "All right," I told him, stretching myself at the mattress's edge. "I'll stay a little while."

He cuddled to me. He wouldn't let go of my hand until he finally drifted to sleep. And right about then, I heard the back door. Samuel coming in. Somehow I'd thought he was already in bed. I rose softly and met him in the kitchen doorway.

"Are we ready for Christmas?" he asked.

"I guess we have to be."

"You've done a good job, Mrs. Wortham." He kissed me.

"You've done a good job too."

Tired as we were, we were both hungry, so I made us some cocoa and sliced a couple of chunks of apple fruit bread.

"I keep expecting George to show up," Samuel told me.

"I'm hoping, I think," I admitted. "I want him to come back for the children's sakes, but I also want him to be in a decent frame of mind, not blind drunk or raging."

"I understand."

We didn't say much else. And it seemed like nearly time to get up by the time we went to bed.

The next morning was Christmas Eve. Bright, sunny. Still white with snow but beautiful. I made oatmeal muffins, and then everybody got ready for special services at church. Before we were part of the Dearing congregation, they'd decided to have services on Saturday whenever Christmas Day fell on a Sunday. They still had services Christmas morning for families close by, but families like ours who lived miles out of town could spend Christmas morning with their families. I was especially glad the Christmas Eve service was in the morning so we wouldn't have to get into town and back in the dark.

We'd finally returned Mr. Post's truck, so young Sam went and hitched his father's team and wagon and drove us all into town bundled under blankets. It was crisp and clear, and we sang Christmas carols on the way. Or at least some of us did. Kirk and Willy and Rorey and Harry had all gone solemn again, but there wasn't anything I knew of to do about it.

Harry was a holy terror in church that morning, absolutely refusing to sit still. He was far from a baby at six years old, but I finally removed him from the sanctuary for a little talking to. But in the hallway, I really didn't have the heart to scold him. How could I expect much different from him? A restless boy on Christmas Eve, thrust in with us after losing one, maybe both, parents? Really, he'd been behaving fairly well considering that. "Can you please be quieter so that other people can enjoy the service?" I asked of him.

"I don't think so," he answered honestly. "I don't think my quiet's workin' very well today."

"Apparently not. Still, it's important that we try. Okay?"

Reluctantly he agreed. And he did manage to make it through the rest of the service with only mild disruption. The pastor didn't seem to mind him slipping down in his seat, fiddling with his sister's hair, or dropping his shoes on the floor in the middle of a prayer. Still, I was relieved when it was time to go home. We presented our gifts to the pastor and his wife before we left, and they were very pleased with them. Juanita hugged me, and for no reason at all I burst into tears.

"Oh, Julia, we're so sorry we haven't been to visit. Are you managing everything all right?"

I nodded, wishing I could find the words to assure her. But Lizbeth found them for me.

"She's been managin' everything real well, Mrs. Pastor. I don't know how she puts up with all a' us, but we appreciate it."

"A lot," young Sam added.

Pastor and Juanita hugged every one of the children, as well as Samuel and me again. We were so blessed to have them, such good friends. I knew they'd been praying for us and would continue to, and that was comfort beyond words for me.

We rode home through the crystal snow, Berty singing his special song again. I joined him at it and then sang "Silent Night" for Katie. She'd gotten so terribly quiet and now was at my side again. I knew she was close to tears, the very nearness of Christmas weighing on her heart with a terrible ache. Why had her mother left her? Didn't she love her? Didn't she care? I'd had those questions when my father went away so long ago, and not even Grandma Pearl could answer them for me. But she'd made Christmas happy anyway. She'd made things seem at least a little all right again. And I hoped, I prayed, that I was doing that for Katie. For all of them.

Something was different as we came up to the house through newly fallen snow. There were tracks across the yard where there'd been none before, and when we got close we could see the back door hanging open as though someone had just rushed in and left it swinging.

Samuel looked at me, but I couldn't read what I saw in his eyes. Young Sam stopped the wagon in the drive and was down off the seat in a flash. Samuel hurried down too. My heart was suddenly thundering. Willy jumped up, and I knew I couldn't stop him or any of the other big boys from rushing inside. But Kirk didn't rush in that direction. He jumped from the wagon and went straight for the barn.

Harry wanted to go in. Everybody else seemed hesitant. But we were home, and it was cold outside. Despite my thundering heart, I rose from the wagon seat, bringing Emmie and a blanket up with me. "We may as well go on inside," I said slowly. "Don't run, all right?"

"Is it Pa?" Franky asked.

Lizbeth looked at me.

"Maybe." That was all I could say. But who else could it be? Samuel's brother Edward coming back to see us? Somehow I doubted that. The last we knew, he was in Tennessee.

Lizbeth bundled a quilt around her shoulders and took Berty's hand. "We oughta go in then."

Joe drew in a deep breath. "I think I'll walk out to the barn with Kirk if you don't mind."

"That would be good," Lizbeth told him.

She and I ushered the young children toward the porch, Katie clinging to my hand like she was scared to death, and Harry stumbling in the snow and rushing ahead.

"I hope he's okay," Franky said softly.

I couldn't even answer. Maybe I was feeling as afraid as Katie was. If it was George, how would he be? Where had he gone? And why? For so long! What had he been thinking?

It was George. Sprawled on our davenport. Samuel and young Sam were just stirring him as we came in, though I would have left him lay.

"Pa!" Harry yelled, rushing forward and destroying their attempt to rouse him gently. Harry jumped on the davenport without hesitation, landing right on his father's legs. Despite Lizbeth's efforts to hold him back, Berty was right behind him, leaping at George's chest before the man managed to sit himself up.

Rorey was a great deal more reserved, standing back with her arms folded.

Willy was too. "Where you been, Pa?"

George just looked around at all of us, his eyes filled with tears. I couldn't tell if he was drunk. I wouldn't have been surprised. He smelled like a sewer rat and looked almost as bad.

"Pa, what happened?" Lizbeth asked more gently.

"I . . . I couldn't do it. I was gonna . . . I was gonna . . ."

135

He looked up at Samuel, seeming almost unable to speak. "I couldn't do it—"

"Do what?" Willy asked. "Leave us for good?"

George looked frightened. Bruised. Filthy. Wherever he'd been, whatever he'd been up to, it hadn't been pleasant. He stared at Samuel. "I remembered . . . the promise . . . last year I promised you . . ."

"Yes, you did," Samuel answered him solemnly. "Need some coffee?"

George nodded. He seemed to be shaking. He had yet to tell us any details of where he'd been, but I figured that had best wait. Till the children were in bed, probably. At least the little ones. It wasn't something they needed to hear. George hugged Berty, who was squeezing his neck. He hugged Harry too. Lizbeth put Emmie in his arms, and he hugged at both of them. Rorey and Willy still hung back. Joe and Kirk hadn't come inside yet. Slowly, George turned his eyes to his oldest son.

"Glad you could make it for Christmas, Pa," young Sam said, his face almost devoid of expression.

"Glad—glad you could make it, boy. I . . . I'm sorry."

I suddenly realized Franky hadn't followed us to the sitting room. When I went to make the coffee and a bite to eat, I found him sitting at the kitchen table with his head down.

"Franky, don't you want to greet your father?"

"Yeah. In a while. When's he's ready. He won't be anxious." He sniffed, and my eyes filled with tears.

"Oh, Franky. Don't you think he wants to see you? He did come back."

136

He nodded, fighting the tears that tried to press at him. "I prayed he would. I'm so glad he did—"

"What's the matter?"

"I . . . I just thought I better wait, that's all, 'fore he sees me."

It broke my heart, seeing Franky's assessment of his father's feelings for him. George was always so hard on him, so impatient, and so cruelly blind to Franky's bright mind, loving heart, and gentle spirit. I couldn't remember ever seeing George extend any affection toward Franky, and Franky clearly didn't expect any now. He felt like the castoff, the least desired, who needed to wait while his father greeted the others before darkening his view. I hoped he was wrong about it, but I just wasn't sure. I'd seen such lack of feeling in George so many times. And yet I knew that Franky loved him anyway.

"Would you like to help me? I'm going to make everyone a sandwich."

He nodded.

Sarah and Katie came and sat at the table, with Katie hugging tight at Sarah's doll. Her face was ashen.

"Everything's all right, honey," I assured her. "Mr. Hammond is home, and we're going to go on with a happy Christmas Eve."

She burst into tears.

"Honey . . ." I took her in my arms, and thankfully Samuel came in the kitchen to make progress with the coffee and sandwiches, or they would never have gotten done.

Katie cried into my blouse, inconsolable. I tried to calm her, but I was helpless to do much of anything except hold

137

her and let the tears flow. Sarah stood beside us the whole time, her hand gently resting on Katie's back.

Samuel and Franky made sandwiches at the table in front of us, but there was nothing I could do but wait with Katie until she could talk to me. I smoothed her hair, I kissed her brow, but nothing seemed to help.

Harry and Bert in the sitting room were loudly telling their father all the things we'd done while he was gone. Lizbeth tried to shush them a little, but it did no good that I could tell. Everyone else in the sitting room seemed painfully quiet, especially George. Until I heard a strange choked sound and realized George was sobbing.

"I don't think he's drunk," Samuel told me. "Not anymore."

"Thank God," I replied.

I carried Katie into the bedroom away from everyone else to try and help her calm down. Only Sarah followed us, and I couldn't refuse her. She shut the door for me, and I sat on the edge of the bed with Katie on my lap.

"Can you tell me what's wrong, honey? Everybody's okay."

She sniffed. She struggled. But finally she could speak. "I—I was scared it was my mommy or—or Uncle Eddie come to take me away."

She sniffed again, wiped her face on the hankie I gave her, and then tried to go on. "But then—then I saw Rorey's daddy." She looked up at me and drew in a sniffly breath. "He—he must love them because—because—he came back—"

I thought I understood. The poor child was torn apart, afraid of her mother taking her away and yet brokenhearted if the woman didn't care enough to come and try. "Honey, I believe your mother loves you."

"No, she doesn't! She won't come! She won't!"

There was nothing I could do but hold her and let her cry some more. What could I say?

Sarah was bold and kind enough to say it for me. "I bet she does love you. She just don't know how to show it. An' we all love you too. I hopes you're feeling better in a minute, 'cause I'm gonna need you."

Katie tried again to dry her eyes. "Why?"

"We got to move Mary and Joseph again, remember? They're supposed to get to Bethlehem today!"

I smiled at my little girl. The culmination of the journey they'd been working on for days was enough to pull Katie out of her sorrow, at least a little.

"Okay. I'll help. Can—can I make Mary walk this time?"

"Yeah. You can move 'em both if you want. And the kings too."

It seemed strange to have George back, but good. A relief to all of us. Rorey warmed up to him slowly, showing him the Christmas angel cookies she'd made for her mother. She hugged him when he offered to take them out to Wila's grave, with a note so that real angels would know where to take them. Willy and Kirk were angry. I knew that and I think their father did too. Sam and Joe shared some of the same feelings, I'm sure, though they were better at keeping them hidden. I understood that Kirk resented his father for being gone without a word and then showing up for Christmas suddenly and expecting everyone to welcome him as though nothing had happened. It was hard to wash all the worries and uncertainty under the bridge.

George seemed to understand that. He gave them space. He apologized. He could hardly seem to keep from crying.

Fortunately we had the children's magical Christmas Eve to take part in. After supper, Sarah wanted Samuel to read the Christmas story, and then she and the other children put it in action right in front of us, using Franky's paper cone figures.

Mary and Joseph proceeded slowly, wearily, to a kitchen chair, where they tried to get lodging but were turned away. They had no choice but to venture to the tabletop, domain of the stable animals, and settle in as best they could. Then Sarah ran frantically upstairs for the baby Jesus. The moment had arrived. But she came tearing right back down again. "Mommy! Mommy! He's gone again!"

I looked around at the other little faces. "Does anyone know where the baby Jesus is?"

Berty looked at Franky with a tiny smile and then confessed. "He's hided in Katie's shoe."

Sarah and Katie ran together to the spot. "You gotta get outta there now!" Sarah exclaimed. "It's time to get borned!"

"Why'd he get in my shoe?" Katie wanted to know.

"He was jus' visitin' you for awhile," Franky explained.

I smiled. Jesus's travels made sense to me now. I'd known very well that Franky hadn't been moving him. I'd asked him about it more than once. But I could well imagine Franky putting Berty up to it, to provide a childish touch of grace on various ones who'd seemed to need it at the time. I marveled at him, cheerfully standing beside his father, though I'd yet to see George acknowledge him directly.

Sarah hurried back to the manger scene with the paper baby cupped in her hand. Katie raced behind her, and the rest of us stayed close enough to watch. Much to his parents' delight, Jesus appeared almost instantly in the manger, and the angels flew like lightning to the far end of the table to tell the shepherds the good news.

Harry and Bert hurried the shepherds and sheep to the baby's side, where Berty soon had them all singing. The angels joined in, even Rorey's crying one, which she perched precariously on the stable's top.

And then Sarah hurried for the wise men.

"Look!" she had one of them exclaim. "See that bright star! It's right over top Bethlehem!"

But the wise men wouldn't reach the manger that night. Sarah and Franky had decided that they must arrive in the morning with their gifts, making our Christmas gift-giving all the more appropriate. Such thinking, however, left Harry with a question.

"If Jesus is borned in the night, why do we have to wait till morning for a present?"

"Because he was borned on Christmas, silly," Rorey said. "You can't stay up till the real part of the night when he was borned. We just know it already happened when we wake up in the morning."

"I wish we could open somethin' tonight," he lamented.

Willy glanced grudgingly at his father. "How you know we even got anythin'?"

George sprung up and fumbled toward the pantry door.

"You do. You do. I—I got the Christmas candy. I couldn't let it go without—without—you know—"

Tears sprung to Lizbeth's eyes. George fumbled about in our pantry. "It's a . . . it's a special occasion," he mumbled. "Samuel, do you think unner the circumstance it'd be all right—"

"Yes," Samuel answered without waiting for George's words to come out right. "It feels like Christmas is already here."

Finally George found what he was looking for. A sack he must have thrown in on a shelf before we got home. The Hammonds' Christmas candy. One long striped red-and-white stick for each child. And this year, he'd even brought extra for the three Wortham children. I could scarcely believe he'd managed to be that thoughtful. This was something he'd been doing for his children for as long as any of them could remember. Most years they didn't have anything else. But Sam and Lizbeth had known it wouldn't quite seem like Christmas without it.

One taste of the candy, and then it was time for bed. It wasn't hard getting the little ones settled tonight. But the older ones still wanted further explanation from their father. So I made them all tea or cocoa and let Willy, Kirk, Sam, Joe, and Lizbeth sit around the table and listen to their father's story.

"I hitched a ride from the blacktop road," he began. "Got all the way to St. Louis. I won't lie to you none. Got liquored up first. Got good and drunk an' stayed that way 'long as I could."

Lizbeth looked down in her lap. Kirk shuffled in his seat

like he really didn't want to hear any more. But they were all quiet as George continued.

"Didn't think I could go on, you know. I thought the city way off'd be the place to be done with everythin'—didn't want none a' you findin' me. Was gonna jump off the river bridge, that's what I had in my mind to do. Leave you in the care a' the Worthams here. Figured you'd be better off."

No one seemed to know what to say. Samuel had been right to worry. It was a miracle that George had made it home.

"What stopped you, Pa?" Joe asked in a voice that barely sounded like himself, his blue-gray eyes shining wet in the lamplight.

"You're gonna think it sounds crazy," George confessed. "I—I couldn't stop thinkin' 'bout you an' Christmas an' all. Was on my way to the bridge. But I went—I went past a big ol' church. Doggone if it weren't the pertiest choir in there I ever heard in my life. All kids too, singing loud enough to hear 'em clear out to the street. I couldn't stand it for thinking a' you back here. I couldn't go on an' do nothin' like I'd thought, an' leave all a' you wonderin'. That promise I made was near to eatin' me up inside." He glanced over at Samuel. "About—'bout bein' here for m' little ones."

"I'm glad," Samuel told him.

"So am I," Joe echoed softly. "I'm real glad you come back, Pa. You made the right choice."

Lizbeth took her father's hand, silent tears streaming down her cheeks. Kirk and Willy sat like stone, staring at George but not saying a word. It was young Sam who spoke up next, his voice far quieter than usual.

"I hope it's settled in your mind, Pa. We need you here, with your family. We need you sober. It'll be all right. We made it a whole year now, Pa, an' we can keep goin'. You can keep on. You're strong. I know you are, or you wouldn't a' made it home."

"It weren't easy," George stammered. "Didn't have much money lef', barely enough for the Christmas candy. But—but I had to get it. Couldn't go no farther without findin' me a candy store. But then I was scared I'd never get back in time. Couldn't find no long ride. Six or eight folks took me partway. Must a' all thought I was crazy, tryin' to hurry 'em down the road in the snow. Last one let me out at the corner by Mueller's field, an' I run. It like to give me a heart attack that there weren't nobody here, till I figured maybe you was gone to church. Couldn't do nothin' but wait. Lordy, it was so good hearin' your voices again, seein' you all lookin' at me . . ."

He leaned his head down in a sob, and I thanked the Lord for touching his heart. Lizbeth kissed his cheek and hugged him. Joe put his arm around him. The others still seemed distant, a little unforgiving, or maybe just uncertain of what to expect now.

Finally Kirk asked a question that could not have been a surprise to anyone. "Why'd you go in the first place, Pa? Maybe us older ones'd make it without you if we had to. But the little kids, Pa—you 'bout broke their hearts. They need you awful bad. An' you knowed that all along."

George looked at his son and answered more honestly than I expected. "Sometimes what I knows gets lost in a fog, boy. Weren't mindful a' them when I lef'. Was only thinkin' 'bout bein' done with the strain a' missin' your mama."

"There ain't no bein' done with that," Kirk replied flatly. "Not for none of us. But you bein' the pa, you oughta be man enough to be here an' do what you can."

George was silent for a moment. I wondered how he'd react. I could almost picture the sobs coming to an abrupt end, replaced by bitter, callous words. But George only bowed his head again. His words were slow and quiet.

"I know it, boy. I know. My pa used to tell me things like that. I oughta be man enough. For this or the other thin'. Funny, though, I never could be. Not man enough for him."

"Pa," Lizbeth said in surprise, "Grandpa Hammond's been gone a lotta years now—"

"I know it. But I still hear his voice sometimes, tellin' me I can't do it. I can't manage to get nothin' right . . . there ain't hardly no use t' tryin' . . ."

Something shook inside me, hearing such words from George. I'd had no idea what his father had been like. I'd never heard much of anything about his parents at all. But these words were so familiar. Didn't George realize the way he passed them on, especially to Franky, who needed his encouragement so badly?

"All you gotta listen to is the present need," young Sam told him. "An' just do what you gotta do. Grandpa ain't 'round no more. You ain't answerin' to him."

George nodded.

"We love you, Pa," Lizbeth whispered.

"I know, girl," George answered her. Silence hung over

everyone, and I felt that it was space just made for George to affirm how much he loved them too. But he didn't say it. His head still bowed, he mumbled barely loudly enough to be heard. "Tomorrow's Christmas. You'all oughta get some sleep."

"In a little while," Lizbeth said softly.

But young Sam stood up. "Prob'ly a good idea."

"I'm sorry," George said to them again. "I know I ain't never got much to give—"

"You bein' here's a gift," Lizbeth answered him. "Especially this Christmas."

"You got a good heart, girl," George said then. "Like your mama."

Lizbeth only nodded, the tears still plain in her eyes. George pulled himself slowly to his feet, and she embraced him. Young Sam followed her lead, but the other boys hung back. And before long, they were all on their way to bed.

Samuel and I lingered in the quiet after they'd turned in. "Thank the good Lord," he whispered to me.

I reached for his hand. "Amen."

It was hard to know what I was feeling inside. A jumble of thoughts and concerns. A strange mix of feelings toward George, especially. I was still bitterly distrusting of him in a way, knowing he'd shown us and his children precious little stability in the past. But I was also heartsick just thinking about him having a father so much like himself, who'd torn him down the way he so often tore down Franky. And he didn't even see it. *Dear God, open his eyes. Help him be a tenderhearted father, even if he had no decent example. Father God, you can be his example, always loving, merciful, and kind.*

Samuel and I finished wrapping our gifts in the butcher paper I'd saved back for the purpose. Then we kissed and went to change for bed. I was just pulling on my nightgown when I heard Berty stirring again in the darkness like he'd done before.

But this time George was close by, on the bed we'd made for him beside the Christmas tree, and he was the one to respond to Berty's cries.

"Stay by my cradle, Pa," I heard the little boy plead.

"Cradle, huh?" George answered. "Didn't think I had no baby boys no more."

"That's any kin' a' bed," Berty explained. "The song says so."

"What song?"

Quietly, in the blackness of night, Berty sang "Away in a Manger" to his father. And George let him sing. It seemed like an answered prayer. I snuggled under the covers with Samuel and smiled.

Till Morning Is Nigh

*M*orning. Christmas. With thirteen children in the house and George among us again. We brought out the presents, and I was so happy to see the smiling faces. George was pleased with the hankies I'd made him. Samuel stunned me by presenting me with a little end table I'd had no idea he was making. And then I had the chance to surprise him with the shirt I'd sewn and hid since harvest when he'd worked so many late hours.

Katie loved her cloth baby doll, and Sarah and Rorey loved the dresses for theirs. They started playing "Christmas" with them right away, and Emmie toddled over to join them with her soft little teddy bear cuddled in her arms. Franky loved the hammer and boards and was ready to start a project immediately. Willy and Robert were just as anxious to go fishing, despite the cold. Even the older children seemed satisfied with their gifts.

I put the turkey in the oven and made cinnamon rolls for breakfast. Then we got the sitting room cleaned up and thought we were pretty much done with Christmas doings besides the happy rest of the day enjoying the dinner to come and one another. But at about 11:30 in the morning we heard a vehicle outside. Pastor and Juanita Jones, bustling in like last year, each of them with an armload. They must have left right after church to come out our way.

Pastor was genuinely surprised to see George but so happy he dropped the bag he was carrying to embrace him.

"Praise the Lord! Praise the Lord!" he exclaimed and then quoted from the story of the prodigal son. "What was dead is alive again. What was lost is found."

They brought a whole sack of sweaters, one for each child. Plus candy canes, divinity, three pies, and a sack of oranges.

"How could you afford all this?"

"We didn't," Juanita told me. "The whole church contributed."

They hugged everybody. We hugged them. They had only meant to deliver the gifts this time and not stay, but I talked them into joining us for Christmas dinner. Sarah, Franky, and the rest acted out the Christmas story with our paper cone manger scene all over again, and the pastor loved it. He credited me with the ingenuity of the whole thing, but I let him know it was Franky's original idea and then it had grown from there.

Katie came back to clinging at my side. Any time I sat

down, she was right on my lap, leaning into me, hugging at my neck. I didn't mind, even when I was in the middle of everything else. After dinner she finally got up the nerve to ask me what must have been working in her mind for quite awhile.

"Mommy's not gonna come, is she? She's never coming back to see me."

"I don't know about never," I said. "I can't imagine her being able to live without seeing you again. But it doesn't look like she'll be here today, sweetie. There's no reason to expect it."

I thought she might cry again. But she didn't.

"If Sarah is my always sister, will you be my always mama?"

"If you want me to."

"I do."

I kissed her forehead. "Then we're family, just like I told you. Always and forever."

She seemed satisfied. She climbed down and went to play with her doll and the other girls again. Juanita smiled at me. "I don't know how you do it."

"I don't," I said softly. "Whatever you think I'm accomplishing, I really can't manage at all. Nothing but the good Lord could have gotten me through this holiday."

"Do you miss Emma?" she asked me.

Dear Emma, who'd given us this farm, introduced us to the Hammonds and our church family, and impacted my life with her wonderful seeds of faith. "Of course. And my mother and father. And Grandma Pearl, and Mrs. Hammond. I even miss Hazel Sharpe in some funny way."

Juanita smiled. "Snippety old Hazel. I loved her too."

It was such a happy Christmas. George had cleaned up and was downright pleasant all day long. None of the children fought or carried on at each other. Much. And I felt so completely blessed, when we'd had next to nothing, for God to make a way for a beautiful Christmas despite all our tears.

We sang carols after dinner while the pastor and Juanita were still there. "Joy to the World." "O Little Town of Bethlehem." "O Come, All Ye Faithful." And of course, "Silent Night" and Berty's favorite, "Away in a Manger."

"Till morning is nigh . . ." he sang out as loudly as he could, holding each note a little longer than it was meant to be held. "What's that mean, anyway?"

"Till the morning comes upon us," the pastor explained. "And the darkness is gone away. I believe that whole line is a prayer for the Lord to be with us through all the tough times, till the final morning when he takes us home, like the last verse says."

I'm not sure Berty understood that, but he seemed to accept it well enough whether he understood or not. He grabbed the paper Jesus, lifted him high, and went twirling around the house, singing at the top of his lungs.

"I love thee, Lor' Jesus! Look down fwom da sky! An' stay by my cradle till morning is nigh!"

Merry Christmas, Berty. And Franky, Sarah, Katie, Lizbeth, and all the rest. Merry Christmas, George. But especially—Merry Christmas, Jesus. Happy Birthday.

"Be near us, Lord Jesus, we ask thee to stay. Close by us forever, and love us, I pray. Bless all the dear children in thy tender care. And take us to heaven to live with thee there."

For Christmases past and present, for your comfort in the time of trial, your salvation, your wonderful promises, and especially for your presence with us as we walk the path of life, we thank you, Lord God. Stay by our cradle. Till morning is nigh.

Amen.

Grandma's Apple Fruit Bread

2½ cups flour	3 eggs
1½ cups sugar	¾ cups cold coffee
½ teaspoon salt	1½ cups raisins
1½ teaspoons baking soda	1½ cups chopped apple
1½ teaspoons cinnamon	1 cup chopped nuts
½ cup lard (or shortening)	

Sift dry ingredients and blend with lard (or shortening). Add unbeaten eggs and beat well. Flour the fruits and nuts before adding. Add coffee alternately with fruit and nuts and stir well. Bake in 2 large loaf pans (greased) at 350 degrees for about 1 hour.

Variation: To make Grandma's Apple Fruit Cake, add 1 teaspoon ground cloves, ½ cup candied cherries, and ¾ cup candied citron. Can also substitute pears for half or more of the apples. Good for family and company.

Date Nut Bread

1 cup dates (chopped)	2 eggs
2 teaspoons baking soda	4 cups flour
2 cups boiling water	1 teaspoon salt
3 tablespoons lard or shortening	2 teaspoons vanilla
1¾ cups sugar	1 cup chopped nuts

Pour boiling water over dates; let cool. Mix with all other ingredients and bake in greased pans at 350 degrees for 50 to 55 minutes. Makes 2 loaves—1 for home, 1 to give away.

Snickerdoodles

1 cup lard or shortening
(part butter or margarine)

1½ cups sugar

2 eggs

2¾ cups flour

2 teaspoons cream of tartar

1 teaspoon baking soda

¼ teaspoon salt

2 tablespoons sugar

2 teaspoons cinnamon

Heat oven to 400 degrees. Mix shortening, 1½ cups sugar, and eggs thoroughly. Sift flour and blend with cream of tartar, baking soda, and salt; stir into mixture. Shape dough into 1-inch balls. Roll in a mixture of 2 tablespoons sugar and the cinnamon. Place 2 inches apart on ungreased baking sheet. Bake 8 to 10 minutes. These cookies puff up at first, then flatten out. Makes 6 dozen.

Christmas Sugar Cookies

¾ cup lard or shortening   2 teaspoons vanilla
¼ cup butter or margarine   3 cups flour
1 cup sugar   1 teaspoon salt
2 eggs   1 teaspoon baking powder

Cream shortening, butter, and sugar. Mix in eggs and vanilla. Mix in other dry ingredients. Roll out on floured surface to ¼-inch thickness or less. Cut into desired shapes, place on ungreased baking sheet, and decorate as desired. Bake at 350 degrees. Remove before browned, about 8 to 10 minutes. Yield will depend upon size of the cookies, usually 6 to 7 dozen. For iced cookies, decorate after baked cookies have cooled.

Leisha Kelly is the author of five popular historical fiction books, including *Julia's Hope*, *Emma's Gift*, *Katie's Dream*, *Rorey's Secret*, and *Rachel's Prayer*. She is also the author of *Tahn*, *Return to Alastair*, and *The Scarlet Trefoil*. She has served many years on her local library board, continuing to bring good reads and educational opportunities to her community. Once a waitress, café manager, tutor, and EMT, Leisha is now a busy novelist and speaker who is active in the ministries of her church. She lives with her family in Clayton, Illinois.

For more information on Leisha and her books, go to www.leishakelly.com.

CROSSINGS®
THE BOOK CLUB FOR TODAY'S CHRISTIAN FAMILY

A Letter to Our Readers

Dear Reader:

In order that we might better contribute to your reading enjoyment, we would appreciate your taking a few minutes to respond to the following questions. When completed, please return to the following:

Andrea Doering, Editor-in-Chief
Crossings Book Club
401 Franklin Avenue, Garden City, NY 11530
You can post your review online! Go to www.crossings.com and rate this book.

Title _____ Author _____

1 Did you enjoy reading this book?

☐ Very much. I would like to see more books by this author!

☐ I really liked_____

☐ Moderately. I would have enjoyed it more if_____

2 What influenced your decision to purchase this book? Check all that apply.

      ☐ Cover
      ☐ Title
      ☐ Publicity
      ☐ Catalog description
      ☐ Friends
      ☐ Enjoyed other books by this author
      ☐ Other _____

3 Please check your age range:

      ☐ Under 18   ☐ 18-24
      ☐ 25-34   ☐ 35-45
      ☐ 46-55   ☐ Over 55

4 How many hours per week do you read? _____

5 How would you rate this book, on a scale from 1 (poor) to 5 (superior)?
_____

Name_____

Occupation_____

Address_____

City_____ State_____ Zip_____